© Dorothy Hong

ABOUT THE AUTHOR

Ben Greenman is an editor at *The New Yorker*. His acclaimed works of fiction include *What He's Poised to Do, Please Step Back, Superbad, Superworse,* and *A Circle Is a Balloon and Compass Both*. His fiction, essays, and journalism have appeared in the *New York Times*, the *Washington Post, The Paris Review, Zoetrope: All-Story, McSweeney's, Opium Magazine,* and elsewhere. Greenman lives in Brooklyn with his wife and two children.

Also by Ben Greenman

Superbad

Superworse

A Circle Is a Balloon and Compass Both

Correspondences

Please Step Back

What He's Poised to Do

CELEBRITY
CHEKHOV

STORIES BY ANTON CHEKHOV

Translated by Constance Garnett

Adapted and Celebritized by Ben Greenman

HARPER ⬤ PERENNIAL

NEW YORK • LONDON • TORONTO • SYDNEY • NEW DELHI • AUCKLAND

HARPER ● PERENNIAL

HarperCollins books may be purchased for educational, business, or sales promotional use. For information please write: Special Markets Department, HarperCollins Publishers, 10 East 53rd Street, New York, NY 10022.

Designed by Justin Dodd

Library of Congress Cataloging-in-Publication Data is available upon request.

ISBN 978-0-06-199049-6

10 11 12 13 14 OV/RRD 10 9 8 7 6 5 4 3 2 1

To all the Russians or part Russians in my family, and to all the people I know who look Russian, or have Russian blood in their veins, or have recently opened a book that uses as its foundation the literature of a great Russian author.

That should cover it.

CONTENTS

INTRODUCTION

THE GREAT AUTHOR AND DRAMATIST ANTON CHEKHOV WAS born on January 29, 1860, in Taganrog, Rostov Oblast, Russia. A hundred years later to the day, in Philadelphia, came the birth of the model Gia Carangi, who would later be memorably portrayed by Angelina Jolie in the HBO original movie *Gia*.

Coincidence? Not unless you let it be. As Chekhov said, "Only entropy comes easy."

Chekhov is well-known for his plays: his towering quartet of late works, *The Seagull*, *Uncle Vanya*, *Three Sisters*, and *The Cherry Orchard*, have ensured that he is second only to Shakespeare among Western dramatists. But his short stories make an equally persuasive case for his genius as a writer. During his lifetime, Chekhov wrote more than two hundred stories, earning a reputation as one of the most incisive and skilled practitioners in the history of the form.

What makes his stories so compelling? The question has pre-occupied scholars and critics, as well as everyday readers, for more than a century. Most of Chekhov's adherents arrive at a version of the same answer: that Chekhov understood people particularly well, and specifically that he understood their weaknesses. With a minimum of flamboyant effects, he demonstrated the ways in which ordinary life is always colored by predictable but consequential personality flaws such as doubt, pride, and fear. In a story like "Tall and Short," for example, he wasted no time in delineating the complex circuit of envy and aggression that exists between two old friends who meet after a long interval. In "An Enigmatic Nature," he sketches a portrait of a woman on a train with brief, almost imperceptible strokes that nevertheless reveal a tremendous amount about sex, power, identity, aging, and regret.

Chekhov drew his characters from all levels of Russian society in his time: peasants, aristocrats, intense young clerks, disappointed wives. Today, in America, we have a simple way of identifying these flawed specimens of humanity ruled by ego and insecurity. They are called "celebrities." Here we have the young film star who has been in the spotlight since she was a teenager and whose sense of herself is at once inflated and imploded. There we have the talk-show host who conducts clandestine relationships with members of his staff. And over there we have the reality-show star who is famous primarily for her appearance in a particularly intimate home movie.

We need not name these three celebrities, but we can certainly speculate. Lindsay Lohan? David Letterman? Kim Kardashian? And, having speculated, we can perhaps find analogues for these characters in Chekhov's stories—and wonder, perchance, what would happen if his original characters were replaced by these new characters, whose travails hit so much closer to home for us. If we should trap these celebrities inside Chekhov's stories, is it possible that their insides—the inner lives that are elided by the tabloids, paparazzi, and the Internet—might be liberated? That a story of straying husbands and nervous wives like "Bad Weather" might move us more as an accurate, even revealing portrait of a contemporary golfer named Tiger rather than the tale of a lawyer named Kvashin? That a tragicomedy of young love like "At the Barber's" might be enhanced if it starred the singer, actor, and stage parent Billy Ray Cyrus rather than the locksmith Erast Ivanitch Yagodov? It should be specified—stressed, even—that the famous personages transplanted into these pages are in no way intended to reflect the actual lives of the actual talk-show hosts, actresses, golfers, and singers whose names they share. No celebrities were harmed in the making of this book. Rather, they are ideas: the notion of "David Letterman," for example, carries with it an expectation of wit, professionalism, and faux-churlishness. How do those expectations bloom, or wilt, in these stories? Turn the page and see.

Some may wonder whether the presence of modern celebrities in these stories could prove distracting rather than illuminating, whether the subtle beauty of Chekhov's insights might be drowned in a tide of pointless associations. At first we shared that concern. We met in several conference rooms, each adjacent to the next, to discuss the matter. In the end we cast our lot with science and commissioned the research arm of the publisher to conduct an in-depth survey. The results, when they came in, suggested that these new celebritized stories will appeal to a wide variety of readers: young and old, literary or obsessed with celebrity, cynical or idealistic. Or, perhaps, that they will not appeal to them. The graph is difficult to read, and it is possible that we are holding it upside down.

Ben Greenman
General Editor
May 2010

TALL AND SHORT

TWO FRIENDS—ONE A TALL WOMAN AND THE OTHER SHORT— met at the airport. The tall woman had just applied her makeup and her lips shone like ripe cherries. She smelled of flowers and citrus. The short woman had just come off the plane and was laden with bundles and bags. She smelled of ham and coffee grounds. An equally short man with closely cropped black hair peaked on top like a wave came into view behind her back, along with a young girl wearing a hat.

"Nicole," cried the tall woman on seeing the short one. "Is it you? My dear girl! How many summers, how many winters!"

"Holy saints!" cried the short woman in amazement. "Paris! The friend of my childhood! Where have you dropped from?"

The friends kissed each other three times and gazed at each other with eyes full of tears. Both were agreeably astounded.

"My dear girl!" began the short woman after the kissing. "This is unexpected! This is a surprise! Come have a good look at me! Just as pretty as I used to be! Good gracious me! Well, and how are you? Married? I am married as you see. This is my husband, Joel, Joel Madden, though I did not take his last name. He's from Good Charlotte, the band, do you remember their albums? And this is my daughter, Harlow. She's a third-grader. This is the friend of my childhood, Harlow. We were girls together!"

Harlow thought a little and took off her hat.

"We were young women together," the short woman went on. "Do you remember how they used to tease you? You were nicknamed Parasite because you seemed to feed off the attention of others, and I was nicknamed Mouse because I was tiny and squeaked when I spoke. We were children! Don't be shy, Harlow. Go nearer to her. And this is my husband, Joel Madden, though I did not take his last name, from Good Charlotte, the band, do you remember them?"

Harlow took refuge behind her mother's back.

"Well, how are you doing my friend?" the tall woman asked, looking enthusiastically at her friend. "How have you been doing since your last reality show? Was it a success?"

"Thank you for asking! I am not sure exactly which show you mean, since I have been in a series of them over the past few years. The ratings have not been what I expect, but that's no great matter! My husband still reconvenes his band, and when my father passed a few years ago, a bit of his money came to us. We didn't get a large portion of the inheritance, but even so, "Running with the Night" and "Penny Lover" helped us get along. Now I am in town to film a pilot for a new series. I'll be living in town for a few months. And what about you? I bet you are overseeing a thriving production company."

"No dear woman, go higher than that," said the tall woman. "I am in consideration to run a television studio."

The short woman turned pale and rigid all at once, but soon her face twisted in all directions in the broadest smile; it seemed as though sparks were flashing from her face and eyes. She squirmed, she doubled together, crumpled up. Her bundles and bags seemed to shrink and crumple up too. Her husband's peak of hair grew taller still; Harlow drew herself up to attention and replaced her hat upon her head.

"Paris, dear, I . . . I'm delighted! The friend, one may say, of youth, and to have turned into such a great woman!"

"Come, come!" The tall woman frowned. "What's this tone for? You and I were friends as girls, and there is no need of this official obsequiousness!"

"Merciful heavens! What are you saying . . . ?" sniggered the short woman, wriggling more than ever. "Your gracious attention is like cool water, so refreshing. This, Paris, is my daughter Harlow, and my husband Joel, from Good Charlotte."

The tall woman was about to make some protest, but the face of the short woman wore an expression of such reverence, sugariness, and mawkish respectfulness that the production-company head was sickened. She turned away from the short woman, giving her a hand at parting.

The short woman pressed three fingers, bowed her whole body, and sniggered. Her husband smiled. Harlow looked away and fingered the brim of her hat. All three were agreeably overwhelmed.

A Transgression

A TALK-SHOW HOST NAMED DAVE LETTERMAN PULLED OVER AT A rest stop on his way home, turned off the radio, and heaved a deep sigh. A week before, as he was leaving his home, he had been approached by a man he knew a little bit, a fellow named Robert, who said to him viciously:

"Wait a second! I'll have your hide for going after interns and assistants. Don't be surprised if a baby shows up unannounced one of these days. How will you explain that to your wife?"

Robert demanded that Dave should put money into the bank in his name. Dave hurried away. In the car, on the way home at the rest stop, a week later, he sighed again and reproached himself for the momentary infatuation which had caused him so much worry and misery.

When he reached his home, he sat down to rest on the door-step. It was almost nine o'clock, and a bit of the moon peeped out from behind the clouds. He was nearly alone; his wife and his son were at a school play, and most of the staff was off for the night. Dave heard a noise that sounded faintly like the cry of a bird. He got up and walked around the house. There, in a basket, he saw something that sent his face into a look of horror as if it were a snake coiling to strike. In a small heated patio at the side of the house lay a bundle. Something oblong in shape was wrapped up in something else—judging by the feel of it, a wadded quilt. One end of the bundle was a little open, and Dave, putting in his hand, felt something damp and warm. He leaped to his feet in horror and looked about him like a criminal trying to escape from a cell.

"He has left it!" he muttered through his teeth, clenching his fists. "Here it lies, my transgression! Holy God!"

He was numb with terror, anger, and shame. What was he to do now? What would his wife, Regina, say if she found out? What would people at the show say? Maybe Biff would dig him in the ribs, guffaw, and say: "I congratulate you! Though your hair is gone, your nerve is still there in full. You are a rogue!" Universities would know his secret now, and probably the intern-placement programs would shut their doors to him. Such incidents always get into the papers, and Dave would be dragged through it over and over again.

Dave went inside and sat. After a minute he went back to the patio and brought the bundle with him. He put it in a corner of the room. At the sound of a car outside, he hurried into a chair and took a newspaper for his lap. He distinctly heard the voice of his wife and son. His son slammed the car door, and he flinched. The baby had only to wake up and begin to cry, and the secret would be discovered. Dave was conscious of an overwhelming desire to run.

"Maybe I can take it somewhere else," he told himself. "To a hospital? To a friend's house? I'll get it in the car before anyone else sees it."

Dave swept up the bundle and quietly went out the side door. His car was blocked in by his wife, so he went down the driveway, toward the road, where another car was parked.

"Awful, awful!" he told himself, trying to assume an air of unconcern. "A talk-show host walking down the driveway with a baby! If anyone sees me, I am through. Where am I going with this baby, anyway? I can't just leave it anywhere. Come to think of it, I don't even know what woman it belongs to. Maybe I'd better take it to a friend's house until I sort this all out. Maybe I'll go over to Martha Stewart's. She's got a soft spot for babies. I'll just leave it there and that'll buy me time."

And Dave made up his mind to take the baby to Martha Stewart's house, which was a short drive away, maybe fifteen minutes.

I hope the baby doesn't scream, he thought as he came alongside the car. Isn't this something? Here I am carrying a human being as though it were a bag of groceries. A human being, alive, with a soul, with feelings like anyone else. Maybe Martha Stewart will find a home for it. Maybe this baby will turn out to be a prominent educator or a musician or a statesman. Now it's under my arm like a package. I don't even have a baby seat. Can I just buckle it in?

As Dave was putting the child into the backseat, he looked up at the sky, which was nearly dark now, with darker patches where the trees were, and it suddenly struck him that he was doing something very cruel and criminal.

I can't do this! he thought. I can't bear it. All I am doing is shifting this poor baby from door to door. It's not its fault that it's been born. It's done me no harm. And what was my role in this? The villain's role. I took my pleasure and the innocent has to pay the penalty. What if I put it at Martha Stewart's door and she sends it to an orphanage, and it grows up among strangers, without love, and it becomes a criminal, or a drunk, or a ne'er do well? I could provide for this child easily. I have money. It is, after all, my flesh and blood.

Dave got in the backseat with the bundle, left the door open so the overhead lamp was illuminated, and opened the bundle. The baby was asleep.

"Asleep!" he murmured. "You little thing. Look, you've got your father's hair: it's like the Isthmus of Panama up there. And he's just sleeping, with no knowledge that it's his own father looking at him! Forgive me for what I am about to do."

Dave blinked and felt a spasm in his cheeks. He wrapped the baby, started the car, and drove away.

If I were a decent, honest man, he thought, I should damn everything, go with this baby to Regina, fall on my knees before her and say: "Forgive me! I have sinned! Torture me, but don't ruin an innocent child. Let's adopt him!" She's a good woman, she'd consent. . . . And then my child would be with me!

He reached Martha Stewart's house before he knew it and sat in the car, still hesitating. His phone was ringing but he didn't answer it. It was probably Regina, wanting to know where he had gone. He imagined himself at home, sitting reading the newspaper while a little boy climbed up on his lap. It had happened before— it could happen again. Or could it? There were reporters, lawyers. Dave took the baby out and got ready to carry it up to Martha Stewart's door. Again he felt his face twitch. "Forgive me," he said. "Don't remember me like this."

He stepped toward the house, but immediately returned back toward the car.

"Damn it all!" he said. "I'll take him, and let people say what they like!"

Dave took the baby and strode rapidly back toward the car.

Let them say what they like, he thought. I'll go at once, fall on my knees and say: "Regina!" She is a good sort, she'll understand. And we'll bring him up. If it's a boy we'll call him Gerard, and if it's a girl we'll call her Dorothy. Harry will love a playmate in the house, and it will be another comfort in our old age.

And he did as he determined. Faint with shame and terror, full of hope and vague rapture, he drove home, walked in the front door, went right to Regina, and set the bundle before her.

"Here!" he said with a sob. "Hear me before you punish. The devil drove me to it."

He jumped up without waiting for an answer and ran away as if he had been burned. He was on the side patio where he had first found the baby.

I'll stay here outside till she calls me, he thought. I'll give her time to recover and to think it over.

He was there still a few minutes later when he saw Steve Martin walking along the edge of the house. Dave tried to ignore him, but Steve Martin waved heartily and opened the side door to the patio.

"Hey there," Steve Martin said. "I have the craziest story. Kenny, this guy who does your tree trimming, does some for me too. He was over at my place right before dinner. All of a sudden he started screaming. I thought he had cut himself. But he said that his baby was with him this afternoon and that he had left it here. It totally did him in. He was in no shape to come back over, couldn't even drive, so I said I'd do it. I've been calling you."

"What? What are you saying?" said Dave.

"I know," Steve Martin said. "I thought Kenny was gay too. Turns out that he got a girl from your house staff pregnant. I forget her name. Anyway, that's why he got his head all turned around and left the baby here."

Glancing at Dave's eyes, which were glaring at him with anger and astonishment, Steve Martin cleared his throat guiltily and went on: "Gee, maybe Kenny didn't want me to say anything. I know you have a strict policy about staff fraternizing with other staff. But maybe he couldn't help it."

"Damn it!" Dave shouted, and he went back into the house.

Regina, amazed and wrathful, was sitting as before, her tearstained eyes fixed on the baby.

"There! there!" Dave muttered with a pale face, twisting his lips into a smile. "It was a joke. It's not my baby. Of course it's not. It's Kenny's. I was joking. Steve Martin is here to pick it up and take it back to its father."

A Lady's Story

Some years ago Justin Timberlake and I were riding toward evening in fall time in Louisiana to get some coffee.

The weather was magnificent, but on our way back from the coffee shop we heard a peal of thunder, and saw an angry black storm cloud coming straight toward us. The storm cloud was approaching us and we were approaching it.

Against the background of it my house and church looked white and the tall poplars shone like silver. There was a scent of rain. We should have gone inside but we stayed out in the front yard. My companion was in high spirits. He kept laughing and talking all sorts of nonsense. He said it would be nice if we could suddenly come upon a medieval castle with turreted towers, with moss on it and owls, in which we could take shelter from the rain and in the end be killed by a thunderbolt.

Then the first wave raced through the front yard, there was a gust of wind, and leaves went round and round in the air. Justin Timberlake laughed and twirled around in the weather.

"It's fine!" he cried. "It's splendid!"

Infected by his gaiety, I too began laughing at the thought that in a minute I should be drenched to the skin and might be struck by lightning.

Standing outside during a storm when one is breathless with the wind and feels like a bird, thrills one and puts one's heart in a flutter. By the time we decided to go inside, the wind had gone down and big drops of rain were pattering on the grass and on the roofs.

One of the front windows was open and needed closing. Justin Timberlake began to turn the handle rapidly. He was trying to beat the storm. I stood in the doorway waiting for him to finish and watching the slanting streaks of rain; the sweetish, exciting scent of wet grass was even stronger in the front hall than in the yard; outside, the storm clouds and the rain made it almost twilight.

"What a crash!" said Justin Timberlake, coming up to me after a very loud rolling peal of thunder, when it seemed as though the sky were split in two. "What do you say to that?"

He stood beside me in the doorway and, still breathless from closing the window so fast, looked at me. I could see that he was admiring me.

"Britney," he said, "I would give anything only to stay here a little longer and look at you. You are lovely today."

His eyes looked at me with delight and supplication, his face was pale. He had not shaven in days, and on his beard were glittering raindrops that, too, seemed to be looking at me with love.

"I love you," he said. "I love you, and I am happy at seeing you. I know you cannot be my wife, but I want nothing, I ask nothing; only know that I love you. Be silent, do not answer me, take no notice of it, but only know that you are dear to me and let me look at you."

His rapture affected me too; I looked at his enthusiastic face, listened to his voice, which mingled with the patter of the rain, and stood as though spellbound, unable to stir.

I longed to go on endlessly looking at his shining eyes and listening.

"You say nothing, and that is splendid," said Justin Timberlake. "Go on being silent."

I felt happy. I laughed with delight and ran through the drenching rain out of the house and then back to it; he laughed too, and, leaping as he went, ran after me.

Both drenched, panting, noisily clattering up the stairs like children, we dashed into the room. My father and sister, who were not used to seeing me laughing and lighthearted, looked at me in surprise and began laughing too.

The storm clouds had passed over and the thunder had ceased, but the raindrops still glittered on Justin Timberlake's beard. The whole evening till suppertime he was singing, whistling, playing noisily with the dog and racing about the room after it, so that he nearly upset the woman who was there cleaning. And at supper he ate a great deal, talked nonsense, and maintained that if you eat fresh cucumbers and then lemon, you will smell like springtime.

When I went to bed I turned on the small lamp beside it and threw my window wide open, and an undefined feeling took possession of my soul. I remembered that I was free and healthy, that I had put some songs at the top of the chart, that I was beloved; above all, that I had charted, had charted, what a feeling that was. Then, huddling up in bed at a touch of cold that reached me from the garden, I tried to discover whether I loved Justin Timberlake or not, and fell asleep unable to reach any conclusion.

And when in the morning I saw quivering patches of sunlight and the shadows of the lime trees on my bed, what had happened the day before rose vividly in my memory. Life seemed to me rich, varied, full of charm. Humming, I dressed quickly and went out downstairs.

And what happened afterward? Why—nothing. Justin Timberlake came to see me from time to time. He quickly became the kind of acquaintance who was charming in Louisiana or Orlando, in a storm, but lost his appeal in Los Angeles, in less dramatic weather. When you pour out iced tea for them in town, it seems as though they are wearing other people's coats. In Los Angeles, too, Justin Timberlake spoke sometimes of love, but the effect was not at all the same as in the country.

In Los Angeles we were more vividly conscious of the wall that stood between us. I had put songs in the chart, and at that time he had not, though he aspired to do so; both of us—I because of my youth and he for some unknown reason—thought of that wall as very high and thick, and when he was with me in Los Angeles he would criticize other chart-topping pop stars' society with a forced smile, and maintain a sullen silence when any of them called or texted me. There is no wall that cannot be broken through, but the heroes of the modern romance, so far as I know them, are too timid, spiritless, lazy, and oversensitive, and are too ready to resign themselves to the thought that they are doomed to failure, that personal life has disappointed them; instead of struggling they merely criticize, calling the world vulgar and forgetting that their criticism passes little by little into vulgarity.

I was loved, happiness was not far away, and seemed to be almost touching me; I went on living in careless ease without trying to understand myself, not knowing what I expected or what I wanted from life, and time went on and on. People passed by me with their love, bright days and warm nights flashed by, the nightingales sang, the grass smelt fragrant, and all this, sweet and overwhelming in remembrance, passed with me as with everyone rapidly, leaving no trace, was not prized, and vanished like mist. Where is it all?

My father is dead, I have grown older; everything that delighted me, caressed me, gave me hope—the patter of the rain, the rolling of the thunder, thoughts of happiness, talk of love—all that has become nothing but a memory, and I see before me a flat desert distance; on the plain not one living soul, and out there on the horizon it is dark and terrible.

A ring at the bell. It is Justin Timberlake. When in the winter I see the trees and remember how green they were for me that one summer, I whisper:

"Oh, my loves!"

And when I see people with whom I spent my youth, I feel sorrowful and warm and whisper the same thing.

Justin Timberlake has been through it too. He put some songs on the chart, and then left off for other pursuits. He looks a little older, a little fallen away. He has long given up declaring his love, has left off talking nonsense, dislikes some of his work intensely, is indifferent to other parts of it, is ill in some way and disillusioned; he has given up trying to get anything out of life, and takes no interest in living. Now he has sat down by the hearth and looks in silence at the fire.

Not knowing what to say, I ask him:

"Well, what have you to tell me?"

"Nothing," he answers.

And silence again. The red glow of the fire plays about his melancholy face.

I thought of the past, and all at once my shoulders began quivering, my head dropped, and I began weeping bitterly. I felt unbearably sorry for myself and for this man, and passionately longed for what had passed away and what life refused us now. And now I did not think about the pop charts.

I broke into loud sobs, pressing my temples, and muttered:

"My God! My life is wasted!"

And he sat and was silent, and did not say to me: "Don't weep." He understood that I must weep, and that the time for this had come.

I saw from his eyes that he was sorry for me; and I was sorry for him, too, and vexed with this man who could not make a life for me, nor for himself.

When I saw him to the door, he was, I fancied, purposely a long while putting on his coat. Twice he kissed my hand without a word, and looked a long while into my tearstained face. I believe at that moment he recalled the storm, the streaks of rain, our laughter, my face that day, he longed to say something to me, and he would have been glad to say it; but he said nothing, he merely shook his head and pressed my hand. God help him!

After seeing him out, I went back to my study and again sat on the carpet before the fireplace. The red embers were covered with ash and began to grow dim. The frost tapped still more angrily at the windows, and the wind droned in the chimney.

The maid came in and, thinking I was asleep, called my name.

BAD WEATHER

BIG RAINDROPS WERE PATTERING ON THE DARK WINDOWS. IT WAS one of those disgusting summer rains which, when they have begun, last a long time. It was surprisingly cold and there was a feeling of raw, unpleasant dampness. The mother-in-law of the golfer Tiger Woods, Barbro Holmberg, and Tiger Woods's wife, Elin Nordegren, dressed in sweaters despite the season, were sitting over the dinner table in the dining room.

It was written on the countenance of the elder lady that she was well-fed, well-clothed, and in good health, that she had married her daughter to a good man, and now could, with an easy conscience, spend time shuffling and dealing from a fortune-teller's deck; her daughter, a beautiful woman in her late twenties, with a gentle face, was reading a book with her elbows on the table;

judging from her eyes she was not so much reading as thinking her own thoughts, which were not in the book. Neither of them spoke. There was the sound of the pattering rain, and from the kitchen they could hear the prolonged yawns of the cook.

Tiger Woods himself was not at home. Many weekends he was playing tournaments in other cities or even distant nations; on those weekends, the damp, rainy weather made his absence seem greater than it was, especially if his tournament was taking place in good weather. This weekend, Tiger Woods was not out of town, but he was not home either. When Tiger Woods was at home during rain, he despised the conditions. He was of the opinion that the sight of the gray sky and the rain on the windows deprived him of energy he needed for golf. This particular weekend, because of the weather, he was at one of his other properties, a ranch in eastern Texas where he could practice all day at a driving range.

After two rounds with the fortune-teller's deck, the old lady shuffled the cards and took a glance at her daughter.

"I have been trying with the cards to determine whether it will be fine tomorrow, and whether Tiger will be home," she said. "He hasn't been here all week."

Elin Nordegren looked indifferently at her mother, got up, and began walking up and down the room.

"The barometric pressure was rising yesterday," she said doubtfully, "but they say it is falling again today."

The old lady laid out the cards in three long rows and shook her head.

"Do you miss him?" she asked, glancing at her daughter.

"Of course."

"I see you do. I should think so. When I visited over the summer he might be out of the house two days in a row, maybe three. But now it is serious. Five days! I am not his wife, and yet I miss him. And yesterday, when I heard that the chance of rain was smaller, I ordered the cook to prepare a Cornish hen and a trout for Tiger. He likes them. Your poor father couldn't bear fish, but Tiger likes it. He always eats it with great relish."

"My heart aches for him," said the daughter. "It is not very exciting here most days, but it is less exciting still without him, you know, Mama."

"I should think so! At the driving range for ten hours, and all by himself at the ranch at night."

"And what is so awful, Mama, is that he's truly alone. He doesn't even keep house staff. There's no one to help him with physical therapy or prepare him food. Why doesn't he keep some-one in Texas full-time? What use is that place at all if it makes him miserable? A year ago I told him that we should sell it, but no, 'You are happy when we come here,' he said, but do I seem happy to you, Mama?"

Looking over her mother's shoulder, the daughter noticed a mistake in the rows of cards, bent down to the table and began correcting it. A silence followed. Both looked at the cards and imagined how Tiger Woods, utterly forlorn, was sitting now in Texas in the large, empty ranch, or driving balls into the hot afternoon sun, hungry, exhausted, yearning for his family. . . .

"Do you know what, Mama?" said Elin Nordegren suddenly, and her eyes began to shine. "If the weather is the same tomorrow, I'll take one of the other planes and go to see him at the ranch! At least I could find out how he is, have a look at him, and make him a meal or two."

And both of them began to wonder how it was that this idea, so simple and easy to carry out, had not occurred to them before. It was only twenty minutes to the airstrip, and then two hours to the ranch. They said a little more, and went off to bed in the same room, feeling more contented.

"Oh, Lord," sighed the old lady when the clock in the hall struck two. "There is no sleeping."

"You are not asleep, Mama?" the daughter asked in a whisper. "I keep thinking of Tiger. I only hope he won't ruin his health in Texas. Where does he eat without a cook? Bars? Fast food? Pancake houses?"

"I have thought of that myself," sighed the old lady. "May the Lord save and preserve him. But the rain, the rain!"

In the morning the rain was not pattering on the panes, but the sky was still gray. The trees stood looking mournful, and at every gust of wind they scattered drops. The footprints on the muddy path, the ditches and the ruts, were full of water. Elin Nordegren made up her mind to go.

"Give him my love," said the old lady, wrapping her daughter up. "Tell him not to think too much about tournaments. And he must rest. Let him wrap his throat up when he goes out: the weather—God help us! And take him the Cornish hen; food from home, even if cold, is better than at a restaurant."

The daughter went away, saying that she would come back that night or else next morning.

But she came back long before dinnertime, when the old lady was sitting in her bedroom and drowsily thinking what to cook for her son-in-law's supper.

Going into the room, her daughter, pale and agitated, sank on the bed without uttering a word or taking off her coat, and pressed her head into the pillow.

"But what is the matter," said the old lady in surprise, "why back so soon? Where is Tiger Woods?"

Elin Nordegren raised her head and gazed at her mother with dry, imploring eyes.

"He is deceiving us, Mama," she said.

"What are you saying? Christ be with you!" cried the old lady in alarm. "Who is going to deceive us? Have mercy on us!"

"He is deceiving us, Mama!" repeated her daughter, and her chin began to quiver.

"How do you know?" cried the old lady, turning pale.

"The ranch is locked up. The man who lives down the road tells me that Tiger has not been there once in these five days. He is not living at home! He is not at home, not at home!"

She waved her hands and burst into loud weeping, uttering nothing but: "Not at home! Not at home!"

She began to be hysterical.

"What's the meaning of it?" muttered the old woman in horror. "He texted you the day before last to say that he has been practicing hard. Where is he sleeping?"

Elin Nordegren felt so faint that she could not take off her hat. She looked about her blankly, as though she had been drugged, and clutched at her mother's arms.

"What a person to trust: the man down the road!" said the old lady, fussing round her daughter and crying. "What a jealous girl you are! He is not going to deceive you, and how dare he? We are not just anybody. I have held public office. You modeled. He has no right, for you are his wife. We can take him to court."

And the old lady herself sobbed and gesticulated, and she felt faint, too, and lay down on her bed. Neither of them noticed that patches of blue had made their appearance in the sky, that the clouds were more transparent, that the first sunbeam was cautiously gliding over the wet grass in the garden, that with renewed gaiety the sparrows were hopping about the puddles that reflected the racing clouds.

Toward evening Tiger Woods arrived. The man down the road had called him to tell him that Elin had come to the ranch.

"Here I am," he said gaily, coming into his mother-in-law's room and pretending not to notice their stern and tearstained faces. "Here I am! It's five days since we have seen each other!"

He rapidly kissed his wife on her lips and his mother-in-law on the cheek, and with the air of a man delighted at having finished a difficult task, he sat down in an armchair.

"So tired," he said, puffing out all the air from his lungs. "What a week. The second I landed in Texas, I got a call from Charles Barkley, who just invested in this massive indoor golf facility in Nevada. I know that you don't like it when I spend time with him, but he said I had to see it. I got right back in the plane. I didn't spend a minute in Texas. And this place was just incredible. It's a huge room, bigger than a football field, with hydraulics under the ground so that the terrain can change to mimic any hole in the world. It was like a wonderland. I got lost in it. It's indoors, so I wasn't even sure if it was day or night. It was like I was in a casino, on some strange kind of bender, except we didn't drink or eat or anything. Only golf. I played so much that I think I might have overdone it."

And Tiger Woods, holding his knee as though it were aching, glanced stealthily at his wife and mother-in-law to see the effect of his lie, or as he called it, diplomacy. The mother-in-law and wife were looking at each other in joyful astonishment, as though beyond all hope and expectation they had found something precious that they had feared was lost. Their faces beamed. Their eyes glowed.

"My dear Tiger," cried the old lady, jumping up, "why am I sitting here? Let me get you something to drink. And are you hungry?"

"Of course he is hungry," cried his wife. "Mama, bring a beer and some olives. Where is the cook to set a table? My goodness, nothing is ready!"

And both of them, frightened, happy, and bustling, ran about the room. The old lady could not look without laughing at her daughter who had slandered an innocent man, and the daughter felt ashamed.

The table was soon laid. Tiger Woods, who smelled of Krystal and cigars and who had been dining at fine restaurants all week, complained of being hungry, forced himself to munch, and kept on talking of Charles Barkley and his investment in the indoor golf facility, while his wife and mother-in-law could not take their eyes off his face, and both thought:

How clever and kind he is! How handsome!

All serene, thought Tiger Woods as he lay down on his bed. They are ordinary people. They bore me, in a way. And yet they have a charm of their own, and I can spend a day or two each week with enjoyment. He wrapped himself up to get warm, and as he dozed off, he repeated to himself, All serene!

THE ALBUM

THE LIEUTENANT GOVERNOR, THIN AND SLENDER AS THE Katmai Peninsula, stepped forward and, addressing Sarah Palin, said:

"Governor! We are moved and touched to the bottom of our hearts by the way you have conducted yourself during your administration, by your two years here. . . ."

"More than two years," prompted the adjutant general.

"Yes. More than two years. During the course of that time, we, on this so memorable for us . . . uh . . . day, want you to accept in token of our respect and profound gratitude this album with our portraits in it, and express our hope that for the duration of your distinguished life, that for long, long years to come, to your dying day you may not forget . . ."

"With your guidance in the path of justice and progress," added the adjutant general, wiping from his brow the perspiration that had suddenly appeared on it; he was evidently longing to speak, and in all probability had a speech ready.

"And," the lieutenant governor wound up, "may you continue to rise on the national scene, insisting on personal responsibility, government accountability, and a return to family values."

A tear trickled down Sarah Palin's cheek.

"Gentlemen!" she said in a shaking voice, "I did not expect this. I had no idea that you were going to celebrate my time here. We are dwarfed by the mountains and the rest of this majestic landscape, but we're like a light burning in the middle of it. I'm so touched. I won't forget this. I'm happy for myself, of course, but I'm sad for the people of Alaska. No one cares more for them than I do. Everything I have done has been for them."

Sarah Palin hugged her lieutenant governor, who would shortly become governor, and the adjutant general, who would become lieutenant governor. She bowed her head to recover the beginning of her speech. Then Sarah Palin made a gesture that signified that she could not speak for emotion, and shed tears as though an expensive album had not been presented to her, but on the contrary, taken from her. Then when she had a little recovered and said a few more words full of feeling and hugged everyone a second time, she went out amid loud and joyful cheers, got into her Suburban, and drove off, followed by their blessings. As she headed home she was aware of a flood of joyous feelings such as she had never known before, and once more she shed tears.

At home new delights awaited her. There, her family, her friends, and acquaintances had prepared her such an ovation that it seemed to her that she really had been of very great service to her state, and that if she had never existed it would perhaps have been in a very bad way. The dinner was made up of toasts, speeches, and tears. In short, Sarah Palin had never expected that her merits would be so warmly appreciated.

"Everyone!" she said before dessert, "two hours ago I was repaid for all the sufferings anyone has to undergo who is the servant, so to say, not of routine, not of the letter, but of duty! Through my entire time as the governor of this great state I have constantly adhered to this principle: the public does not exist for us, but we for the public, and today I received the highest reward! I was presented with an album. See! I was touched."

Festive faces bent over the album and began examining it.

"It's a pretty album," said Sarah Palin's daughter Piper, "it must have cost a hundred dollars, at least. I love it! You must give me the album, Mama, do you hear? I'll take care of it, it's so pretty."

After dinner Piper carried off the album to her room and shut it up in her table drawer. Next day she took the pictures of the lieutenant governor and the adjutant general out of it, flung them on the floor, and put her school friends in their place. The government dress made way for sweaters and dresses. Piper picked up the pictures of the lieutenant governor and adjutant general and drew flowers growing out of their heads. One man had a moustache; she added one to the other. Neither man had a tiara, and then both did. When there was nothing left to draw she cut the men out of the pictures and taped them to each other, side by side, like paper dolls. Then she carried them to her mother, who was sitting in the office, reading.

"Mama, look!"

Sarah Palin burst out laughing, lurched forward, and, looking tenderly at Piper, gave her a warm kiss on the cheek.

"That's great, baby, go show Daddy; let Daddy see too."

In the Graveyard

THE WIND IS HOWLING, AND IT'S GETTING DARK. SHOULDN'T WE get out of here?"

The wind was frolicking among the yellow leaves of the old birch trees, and a shower of thick drops fell upon us from the leaves. One of our party slipped on the soil and steadied himself on a headstone.

"'Bernard Herrmann,'" he read. "You know who that is, right? A great composer. He did the music to *Citizen Kane*, you know. *Citizen Kane*. And then all the finest Hitchcocks: *Psycho, Vertigo, The Man Who Knew Too Much*. You know that movie *The Day the Earth Stood Still*? It was his, one of the first soundtracks to use electronic effects. I can't believe he's here in the ground. You'd think he had no reason to die. But fate got him. He wasn't even that old. Look at the dates on the stone: he was in his mid-sixties. He had just finished work on *Taxi Driver* and he died in his sleep. His heart just stopped. Now he's here, under this stone, a man whose life was filled with every imaginable kind of sound—joyous, terrifying, romantic— and he's sentenced to eternal silence. Wait. Someone's coming."

A man in a shabby overcoat and apple cap, with a shaven, bluish-crimson countenance, overtook us. He had a bottle under his arm and a magazine was sticking out of his pocket.

"Where is the grave of Andy Kaufman, the comedian?" he asked us in a husky voice.

We conducted him toward the grave of Andy Kaufman, the comedian, who had died years before.

"You are a fan, I suppose?" we asked him.

"No, a comedian, too. Artie Lange," he said, extending his hand. "Though I can see why you'd mistake me for a fan. These days it's hard to tell the difference between comedians and normal people. But hey, I don't mind if the normal people don't."

It was with difficulty that we found the comedian's grave. It had sunken a bit, had a tree overhanging its right half, and was chipped at the top left corner. The Hebrew inscription across the top, covered with green moss blackened by the frost, had an air of aged dejection and looked, as it were, ailing.

" '. . . beloved son, brother, and grandson . . .' " we read.

At the bottom, the words WE LOVE YOU VERY MUCH were still clearly visible.

"Back in the mid-eighties, a bunch of comedians and actors were going to build some kind of monument for him in Los Angeles, but they snorted up the money. . . ." sighed Artie Lange, bowing down to the ground and touching the wet earth with his knees and his cap.

"How do you mean, snorted it?"

"Simple. They collected the money, published a paragraph about it in the newspaper, and spent it on nose candy. I don't say it to blame them. Who am I to judge? They may have thought they did right by him. I wasn't there. I wish them well. I hope his memory lives forever."

"Eternal memory is nothing but sadness. We get remembered for a time, but eternal memory—what next!"

"You are right there. Andy was well-known; there were dozens of baskets sent to his parents, if not hundreds, when he died. He is already mostly forgotten. To some, I mean: those who loved him have let his memory fade so it is no longer painful, but those to whom he did harm remember him. I, for instance, shall never, never forget him, for I got nothing but harm from him. I have no love for the man."

"What harm did he do you?"

"Great harm," sighed Artie Lange, and an expression of bitter resentment overspread his face. "To me he was a villain and a scoundrel. It was through looking at him and listening to him that I became a comedian. By his comedy he lured me from the

parental home, he enticed me with the excitements of the comedian's life, promised me all sorts of things—and brought tears and
sorrow. . . .

"A comedian's lot is a bitter one! I have lost my youth, my hope,
my sobriety. You know how they say that man is made in God's
image? Well, in that case, I feel sorry for the guy, no matter how
all-powerful he is. And money? I have made a little here and there,
but I've lost as much. Look at these shoes. This coat is patched.
My face looks like it's been gnawed by dogs. But don't judge a
book by its cover. That can't even compare to the damage he did
on the inside. My mind is full of freethinking and nonsense. He
robbed me of any faith except the faith in comedy. It would have
been something if I had been able to change the world, but I am
ruined for nothing.

"Damn, it's cold. Want some whiskey? Here. There's enough to
go around. Let's drink to Andy's soul, or however much of it is left.
Though I don't like him and though he's dead, he was the only one
I had in the world, the only one. This is the last time I shall visit
him. I'm not sure how much longer I'll last, so here I have come to
say good-bye. One must forgive one's enemies."

We left Artie Lange to converse with Andy Kaufman and went
on. It began drizzling a fine cold rain.

At the turning into the principal avenue strewn with gravel,
we met a funeral procession. The bearers, wearing black suits and
muddy high boots with leaves sticking on them, carried the brown

coffin. It was getting dark and they hastened, stumbling, and shaking their burden.

"We've only been walking here for a couple of hours and that is the third new arrival we've seen. Shall we go home, friends?"

THE DARLING

Nicole Kidman was sitting on her back porch, lost in thought. It was hot, the flies were everywhere, and she thought to herself that it would soon be evening. The thought pleased her. Dark rain clouds were gathering from the east, and bringing from time to time a breath of moisture in the air.

Tom Cruise, who managed an outdoor theatre in town, was standing in the middle of the garden looking at the sky.

"Again!" he observed despairingly. "It's going to rain again! Rain every day, as though to spite me. I might as well hang myself! It's ruin! Fearful losses every day."

He flung up his hands and went on, addressing Nicole Kidman:

"There! That's the life we lead, Nicole Kidman. It's enough to make one cry. One works and does one's utmost, one wears oneself out, getting no sleep at night, and racks one's brain what to do for the best. And then what happens? To begin with, one's public is ignorant, boorish. I give them the very best operetta, a dainty masque, first rate music-hall artists. But do you suppose that's what they want! They don't understand anything of that sort. They want a clown; what they ask for is vulgarity. And then look at the weather! Almost every evening it rains. It started on the tenth of May, and it's kept it up all May and June. It's simply awful! The public doesn't come, but I've to pay the rent just the same, and pay the artists."

The next evening the clouds would gather again, and Tom Cruise would say with an hysterical laugh:

"Well, rain away, then! Flood the garden, drown me! Damn my luck in this world and the next! Let the artists have me up! Send me to prison!—to the scaffold—to the moon! Ha, ha, ha!"

And next day the same thing.

Nicole Kidman listened to Tom Cruise with silent gravity, and sometimes tears came into her eyes. In the end his misfortunes touched her; she grew to love him. He was a small thin man, with a yellow face, and bangs combed forward on his forehead. He spoke in a thin tenor; as he talked his mouth worked on one side, and there was always an expression of despair on his face; yet he aroused a deep and genuine affection in her.

She was always fond of someone, and could not exist without loving. In earlier days she had loved her papa, who now sat in a darkened room, breathing with difficulty; she had loved her aunt who used to come every other year from Australia; and before that, when she was at school, she had loved her English master. She was a gentle, softhearted, compassionate girl, with mild, tender eyes and very good health. At the sight of her full rosy cheeks, her soft white neck with a little dark mole on it, and the kind, naïve smile, which came into her face when she listened to anything pleasant, men thought, Yes, not half bad, and smiled too, while lady visitors could not refrain from seizing her hand in the middle of a conversation, exclaiming in a gush of delight, "You darling! You pet!"

The house in which she had lived from her birth upward, and which was left her in her father's will, was at the extreme end of the town, not far from the theatre. In the evenings and at night she could hear the band playing, and the crackling and banging of fireworks, and it seemed to her that it was Tom Cruise struggling with his destiny, storming the entrenchments of his chief foe, the indifferent public; there was a sweet thrill at her heart, she had no desire to sleep, and when he returned home at daybreak, she tapped softly at her bedroom window, and showing him only her face and one shoulder through the curtain, she gave him a friendly smile. . . .

He proposed to her, and they were married. And when he had a closer view of her neck and her plump, fine shoulders, he threw up his hands, and said:

"You darling!"

He was happy, but as it rained on the day and night of his wedding, his face still retained an expression of despair.

They got on very well together. She used to sit in his office, to look after things in the theatre, to put down the accounts and pay the wages. And her rosy cheeks, her sweet, naïve, radiant smile, were to be seen now at the office window, now in the refreshment bar or behind the scenes of the theatre. And already she used to say to her acquaintances that the theatre was the chief and most important thing in life and that it was only through the drama that one could derive true enjoyment and become cultivated and humane.

"But do you suppose the public understands that?" she used to say. "What they want is a clown. Yesterday we put on a serious play and almost all the boxes were empty; but if Tom Cruise and I had been producing some vulgar thing, I assure you the theatre would have been packed. Tomorrow Tom Cruise and I are doing a very substantial work. Do come."

And what Tom Cruise said about the theatre and the actors she repeated. Like him she despised the public for their ignorance and their indifference to art; she took part in the rehearsals, she corrected the actors, she kept an eye on the behavior of the musicians, and when there was an unfavorable notice in the local paper, she shed tears, and then went to the editor's office to set things right.

The actors were fond of her and used to call her "Tom Cruise and I," and "the darling"; she was sorry for them and used to lend them small sums of money, and if they deceived her, she used to shed a few tears in private, but did not complain to her husband.

They got on well in the winter too. They took the theatre in the town for the whole winter, and let it for short terms to another traveling company, or to a conjurer, or to a local dramatic society. Nicole Kidman grew stouter, and was always beaming with satisfaction, while Tom Cruise grew thinner and yellower, and continually complained of their terrible losses, although he had not done badly all the winter. He was accustomed to being an active man, and so long as he was inactive, he seemed as though he was wilting. He used to cough at night, and she used to give him hot raspberry tea or lime-flower water, to rub him with eau de cologne and to wrap him in her warm shawls.

"You're such a sweet pet!" she used to say with perfect sincerity, stroking his hair. "You're such a pretty dear!"

Toward Lent he went to the city to collect a new troupe and hike in the mountains, and without him she could not sleep, but sat all night at her window, looking at the stars, and she compared herself with the hens, who were awake all night and uneasy when the cock was not in the henhouse. Tom Cruise wrote once to say that he had scaled one mountain and was about to take a second, adding some instructions about the theatre.

Then came a period of weeks without word, and then one Sunday, late in the evening, a ominous knock at the gate. It persisted and intensified; someone was hammering on it as though they meant to break it. The cook went flopping drowsily toward the gate; Nicole Kidman overtook her and hurried to answer the knock.

"Please open," said someone outside in a thick bass. "There is a telegram for you."

Nicole Kidman had received telegrams from her husband before, but this time for some reason she felt numb with terror. With shaking hands she opened the telegram and read as follows:

TOM CRUISE MISSING. NO BLIZMAN NEWS FOR WEEKS.

FUFUNERAL TUESDAY.

That was how it was written in the telegram—"fufuneral," and the utterly incomprehensible word "blizman." It was cosigned by the stage manager of the theatre company and one of Tom Cruise's hiking guides.

"My darling!" sobbed Nicole Kidman. "My darling! Why did I ever meet you? Why did I know you and love you? Your poor heartbroken Nicole Kidman is alone without you!"

The funeral took place on Tuesday in the city. Nicole Kidman returned home on Wednesday, and as soon as she got indoors, she threw herself on her bed and sobbed so loudly that it could be heard next door, and in the street.

"Poor darling!" the neighbours said as they crossed themselves. "Nicole Kidman, poor darling! How she does take on!"

Three months later Nicole Kidman was coming home from mass, melancholy and in deep mourning. It happened that one of her neighbors, Keith Urban, walked back beside her. He was the manager at the local lumberyard who sang a bit. He wore a fringed jacket, boots, and a gold watch chain, and looked more a man on a stage than a man in trade.

"Everything happens as it is ordained, Nicole Kidman," he said gravely, with a sympathetic note in his voice, "and if any of our dear ones die, it must be because it is the will of God, so we ought have fortitude and bear it submissively."

After seeing Nicole Kidman to her gate, he said good-bye and went on. All day afterward she heard his sedately dignified voice, and whenever she shut her eyes she saw his honey-colored hair. She liked him very much. And apparently she had made an impression on him too, for not long afterward an elderly lady, with whom she was only slightly acquainted, came to drink coffee with her, and as soon as she was seated at the table began to talk about Keith Urban, saying that he was an excellent man whom one could thoroughly depend upon, and that any girl would be glad to marry him.

Three days later Keith Urban came himself. He did not stay long, only about ten minutes, and he did not say much, but when he left, Nicole Kidman loved him—loved him so much that she lay awake all night in a perfect fever, and in the morning she sent for the elderly lady. The match was quickly arranged, and then came the wedding.

Keith Urban and Nicole Kidman got on very well together when they were married.

Usually he sat in the office till dinnertime, then he went out on business, while Nicole Kidman took his place, and sat in the office till evening, making up accounts and booking orders.

"Lumber gets more expensive every year; the price rises twenty percent," she would say to her customers and friends. "Only fancy we used to sell local timber, and now Keith Urban always has to go for wood to the next town over. And the freight!" she would add, covering her cheeks with her hands in horror. "The freight!"

It seemed to her that she had been in the timber trade for ages and ages, and that the most important and necessary thing in life was timber; and there was something intimate and touching to her in the very sound of words such as "baulk," "post," "beam," "pole," "scantling," "batten," "lath," "plank," etc.

At night when she was asleep she dreamed of perfect mountains of planks and boards, and long strings of trucks, carting timber somewhere far away. She dreamed that a whole regiment of six-inch beams forty feet high, standing on end, was marching upon the timber yard; that logs, beams, and boards knocked together with the resounding crash of dry wood kept falling and getting up again, piling themselves on each other.

Nicole Kidman cried out in her sleep, and Keith Urban said to her tenderly: "Nicole Kidman, what's the matter, darling?"

Her husband's ideas were hers. If he thought the room was too hot, or that business was slack, she thought the same. Her husband did not care for entertainments, and on holidays he stayed at home. She did likewise.

"You are always at home or in the office," her friends said to her. "You should go to the movies, darling, or to the circus."

"Keith Urban and I have no time to go to the movies," she would answer sedately. "We have no time for entertainment except for country music. What's the use of these theatres?"

On Saturdays, Keith Urban and she used to go to the evening service; on holidays to early mass, and they walked side by side with softened faces as they came home from church. There was a pleasant fragrance about them both, and her silk dress rustled agreeably. At home they drank tea, with fancy bread and jams of various kinds, and afterward they ate pie. Every day at twelve o'clock there was a savory smell of beet-root soup and of mutton or duck in their yard, and on fast-days of fish, and no one could pass the gate without feeling hungry. In the office the samovar was always boiling, and customers were regaled with tea and cracknels. Once a week the couple went to the baths and returned side by side, both red in the face.

"Yes, we have nothing to complain of, thank God," Nicole Kidman used to say to her acquaintances. "I wish everyone were as well off as Keith Urban and I."

When Keith Urban went away to buy wood or to tour, she missed him dreadfully, lay awake and cried. Sometimes in the evening she used to see a young man named Brad Pitt, to whom they had let their lodge. At length, after these chance meetings had occurred enough times that they no longer seemed random, she began to engage him in conversation, as he had a pleasant face and a curiosity about many matters that also interested her. He started to talk to her about architecture and activism and play cards with her, and this entertained her in her husband's absence. She was particularly interested in what he told her of his home life. He was married and had a number of small children—sometimes he said three, sometimes he rolled his eyes and said that three was just an approximation, and that the actual total might be six or seven—but was separated from his wife because he suspected she had been unfaithful to him, and now he was impatient with her and the children in ways that saddened him. And hearing of all this, Nicole Kidman sighed and shook her head. She was sorry for him.

"Well, God keep you," she used to say to him at parting. "Thank you for coming to cheer me up, and may you have your health."

And she always expressed herself with the same sedateness and dignity, the same reasonableness, in imitation of her husband. As Brad Pitt was disappearing behind the door below, she would say:

"You know, Brad Pitt, you'd better make it up with your wife. You should forgive her for the sake of your children. You may be sure the little ones understand."

And when Keith Urban came back, she told him in a low voice about the young man and his unhappy home life, and both sighed and shook their heads and talked about the children, who, no doubt, missed their father, and by some strange connection of ideas, they bowed to the ground before them and prayed that God would give them children. Though those prayers were not answered directly, for six years the couple lived quietly and peaceably in love and complete harmony.

But one winter day after drinking hot tea in the office, Keith Urban went out into the yard without his cap on to see about sending off some timber, caught cold, and was taken ill. He had the best doctors, but he grew worse and died after four months' illness. And Nicole Kidman was a widow once more.

"I've nobody, now you've left me, my darling," she sobbed, after her husband's funeral. "How can I live without you, in wretchedness and misery! Pity me, good people, all alone in the world!"

She went about dressed in black and without makeup. She hardly ever went out, except to church, or to her husband's grave, and led the life of a nun. It was not till six months later that she opened the shutters of the windows. She was sometimes seen in the mornings, going with her cook to market for provisions, but what went on in her house and how she lived now could only be surmised.

And yet, there was evidence to assist in this surmise. For one, there was the sudden reappearance of Brad Pitt, who came by now regularly to drink tea with Nicole Kidman and read the newspaper aloud to her. There was also the fact that, meeting a lady she knew at the post office, Nicole Kidman said to her: "There is no proper planning for buildings in our town, and that's the cause of all sorts of problems. One is always hearing of a foundation that sinks into the snow, or a roof that is torn off by wind. The fitness of domestic buildings ought to be as important as that of people."

This was clearly an opinion she had acquired from Brad Pitt, though she claimed it as her own. It was evident that she could not live a year without some attachment, and had found new happiness in the lodge. In anyone else this would have been censured, but no one could think ill of Nicole Kidman; everything she did was so natural. Neither she nor Brad Pitt said anything to other people of the change in their relations, and tried, indeed, to conceal it, but without success, for Nicole Kidman could not keep a secret. When he had visitors, and she poured out tea or served the supper, she would begin talking of gables, of levees, or missions to treat onchocerciasis. Brad Pitt was dreadfully embarrassed, and when the guests had gone, he would seize her by the hand and hiss angrily:

"I've asked you before not to talk about what you don't understand. When we actors who enjoy architecture and activism are talking among ourselves, please don't put your word in. It's really too much."

And she would look at him with astonishment and dismay, and ask him in alarm: "But, Brad, what am I to talk about?"

And with tears in her eyes she would embrace him, begging him not to be angry, and they were both happy.

But this happiness did not last long. Brad Pitt departed for what he said was a distant place. And Nicole Kidman was left alone.

Now she was absolutely alone. Her father had long been dead, and his armchair lay in the attic, covered with dust and lame of one leg. She got thinner and plainer, and when people met her in the street they did not look at her as they used to, and did not smile to her; evidently her best years were over and left behind, and now a new sort of life had begun for her, which did not bear thinking about. In the evening Nicole Kidman sat in the porch, and heard the band playing and the fireworks popping in the theatre, but now the sound stirred no response. She looked into her yard without interest, thought of nothing, wished for nothing, and afterward, when night came on she went to bed and dreamed of her empty yard. She ate and drank as it were unwillingly.

And what was worst of all, she had no opinions of any sort. She saw the objects about her and understood what she saw, but could not form any opinion about them, and did not know what to talk about. And how awful it is not to have any opinions! One sees a bottle, for instance, or the rain, or a man driving in his car, but what the bottle is for, or the rain, or the man, and what is the meaning of it, one can't say, and could not even for ten thousand dollars. When she had Tom Cruise, or

Keith Urban, or Brad Pitt, Nicole Kidman could explain everything, and give her opinion about anything you like, but now
there was the same emptiness in her brain and in her heart as
there was in her yard outside. And it was as harsh and as bitter
as wormwood in the mouth.

Little by little the town grew in all directions. The road
became a street, and where the theatre and the timber yard had
been, there were new turnings and houses. How rapidly time
passes! Nicole Kidman's house grew dingy, the roof got rusty, the
shed sank on one side, and the whole yard was overgrown with
docks and stinging nettles. Nicole Kidman herself had grown
plainer and older; in summer she sat in the porch, and her soul, as
before, was empty and dreary and full of bitterness. In winter she
sat at her window and looked at the snow. When she caught the
scent of spring, or heard the chime of the church bells, a sudden
rush of memories from the past came over her, there was a tender
ache in her heart, and her eyes brimmed over with tears; but this
was only for a minute, and then came emptiness again and the
sense of the futility of life. The black kitten rubbed against her
and purred softly, but Nicole Kidman was not touched by these
feline caresses. That was not what she needed. She wanted a love
that would absorb her whole being, her whole soul and reason—
that would give her ideas and an object in life, and would warm
her old blood. And she would shake the kitten off her skirt and
say with vexation:

"Get along; I don't want you!"

And so it was, day after day and year after year, and no joy, and no opinions. Whatever the cook said, she accepted.

One hot July day, toward evening, just as the cattle were being driven away and the whole yard was full of dust, someone suddenly knocked at the gate. Nicole Kidman went to open it herself and was dumbfounded when she looked out: she saw Brad Pitt, grayer and dressed more plainly. She suddenly remembered everything. She could not help crying and letting her head fall on his breast without uttering a word, and in the violence of her feeling she did not notice how they both walked into the house and sat down.

"My dear Brad Pitt! What fate has brought you?" she muttered, trembling with joy.

"It is good to see you, Nicole Kidman," he told her. "I have retired from both acting and from thinking about architecture, and moved back to this part of the country. I am reconciled with my wife, you know."

"Where is she?" asked Nicole Kidman.

"She's in the city with the kids. I have come here to look for lodgings for my youngest son, a place where he can stay while he goes to school."

"Good gracious, my dear soul! Lodgings? Why not have my house? Why shouldn't that suit him? Why, my goodness, I wouldn't take any rent!" cried Nicole Kidman in a flutter, beginning to cry again. "He can live here, and then I will get to see you at times, when you bring him or pick him up. Permit me that kind-ness, at least. Oh dear! How glad I am!"

Next day the roof was painted and the walls were whitewashed, and Nicole Kidman, with her arms akimbo, walked about the yard giving directions. Her face was beaming with her old smile, and she was brisk and alert as though she had waked from a long sleep. Brad Pitt's wife arrived—a beautiful lady with full lips and a pee-vish expression. With her was her little boy, who was ten although small for his age. And scarcely had the boy walked into the yard when he ran after the cat, and at once there was the sound of his gay, joyous laugh.

"Is that your cat?" he asked Nicole Kidman. "When she has little ones, can I have a kitten?"

Nicole Kidman talked to him and gave him tea. Her heart warmed and there was a sweet ache in her bosom, as though he had been her own child. And when he sat at the table in the evening, going over his lessons, she looked at him with deep tenderness and pity as she murmured to herself:

"You pretty pet! . . . My precious! . . . Such a fair little thing, and so clever."

"'An island is a piece of land which is entirely surrounded by water,'" he read aloud.

"An island is a piece of land," she repeated, and this was the first opinion to which she gave utterance with positive conviction after so many years of silence.

Brad Pitt's son began going to the school. His mother departed to visit her father overseas. His father used to go off every day and would often be away from home for three days together, and it seemed to Nicole Kidman as though the boy was entirely abandoned, that he was not wanted at home, that he was being starved, and she carried him off to her lodge and gave him a little room there.

And for six months the boy lived in the lodge with her. Every morning Nicole Kidman came into his bedroom and found him fast asleep, sleeping noiselessly with his hand under his cheek. She was sorry to wake him.

"Come," she would say mournfully, "get up, darling. It's time for school."

He would get up, dress, and say his prayers, and then sit down to breakfast, drink two glasses of juice, and eat a bagel or an apple. All this time he was hardly awake and a little ill-humoured in consequence.

"You don't quite know your math," Nicole Kidman would say, looking at him as though he were about to set off on a long journey. "What a lot of trouble I have with you! You must work and do your best, darling, and obey your teachers."

"Oh, do leave me alone!" the boy would say.

Then he would go down the street to school, a little figure, wearing a big cap and carrying a satchel on his shoulder. Nicole Kidman would follow him noiselessly. When he reached the street where the school was, he would feel ashamed of being followed by

Nicole Kidman, he would turn round and say, "You'd better go home. I can go the rest of the way alone."

She would stand still and look after him fixedly till he had disappeared at the school gate.

Ah, how she loved him! Of her former attachments not one had been so deep; never had her soul surrendered to any feeling so spontaneously, so disinterestedly, and so joyously as now that her maternal instincts were aroused. For this little boy with the dimple in his cheek and the big school cap, she would have given her whole life, she would have given it with joy and tears of tenderness. Why? Who can tell why?

When she had seen the last of the boy, she returned home, contented and serene, brimming over with love; her face, which had grown younger during the last six months, smiled and beamed; people meeting her looked at her with pleasure.

"Good morning, Nicole Kidman. How are you, darling?"

"The lessons are not difficult, but they load the students down with homework," she would relate at the market. "In the first class yesterday they gave him some algebra and also Spanish. You know it's too much."

And she would begin talking about the teachers, the lessons, and the school books.

At three o'clock they had dinner together. In the evening they learned their lessons together and cried. When she put him to bed, she would stay a long time murmuring a prayer; then she would go to bed and dream of that faraway misty future when the boy would finish his studies and become a doctor or an engineer, would have a big house of his own, would get married and have children. . . . She would fall asleep still thinking of the same thing, and tears would run down her cheeks from her closed eyes, while the black cat lay purring beside her: "Mrr, mrr, mrr."

Suddenly there would come a loud knock at the gate.

Nicole Kidman would wake up breathless with alarm, her heart throbbing. Half a minute later would come another knock.

It must be a telegram, she would think, beginning to tremble from head to foot. The boy's mother is sending for him. Oh, mercy on us!

She was in despair. Her head, her hands, and her feet would turn chill, and she would feel that she was the most unhappy woman in the world. But another minute would pass, voices would be heard: it would turn out to be Brad Pitt arriving for one of his short stays.

Well, thank God! she would think.

And gradually the load in her heart would pass off, and she would feel at ease. She would go back to bed thinking of the boy, who lay sound asleep in the next room, sometimes crying out in his sleep:

"I'll give you a piece of my mind! Get away! Shut up!"

HUSH

EMINEM, A WRITER OF HIP-HOP RECORDS, RETURNS HOME LATE at night, grave and anxious, with a peculiar air of concentration. He looks like a man expecting a police raid or contemplating suicide. Pacing about his rooms, he halts abruptly, ruffles up his hair, and says in the tone in which Laertes announces his intention of avenging his sister: "Shattered, soul-weary, misery on my heart, and then to sit down and write. And this is life! Nobody has described the agonizing pain in the soul of a writer who has to amuse the crowd when his heart is heavy or to shed tears on command when his heart is light. I must be playful, coldly unconcerned, witty, but what if I am weighed down with misery, what if I am ill, or my child is dying?"

He says this, brandishing his fists and rolling his eyes. Then he goes into the bedroom and wakes his wife.

"Kim," he says, "I am sitting down to write. Please don't let anyone interrupt me. I can't write with children crying or cooks snoring. See, too, that there's tea and bacon or something. You know that I can't write without tea. It's the one thing that gives me the energy for my work."

Returning to his room, he takes off his coat and boots. He does this very slowly; then, assuming an expression of injured innocence, he sits down to his table.

There is nothing casual, nothing ordinary, on his writing table, down to the smallest trifle, everything bears the stamp of a stern, deliberately planned program. Little busts and photographs of distinguished rappers, heaps of paper filled with scribbles, part of a skull by way of an ashtray, a sheet of newspaper folded carelessly, but so that a passage is uppermost, boldly marked in blue pencil with the word "disgraceful." There are a dozen sharpened pencils, so that no accidental breaking of a point may for a single second interrupt the flight of his creative fancy.

Eminem throws himself back in his chair, and closing his eyes concentrates on his subject. He hears his wife shuffling about in her slippers and lighting the burner beneath the teapot. She is hardly awake; that is apparent from the way she fumbles the knob of the stove. Soon the hissing of the teapot and the spluttering of bacon reaches him.

All at once Eminem starts, opens frightened eyes, and begins to sniff the air.

"Is that gas?" he groans, grimacing with a face of agony. "That woman will kill me yet. How in God's name am I supposed to write in such surroundings, kindly tell me that?"

He rushes into the kitchen and breaks into a theatrical wail. When a little later his wife, stepping cautiously on tiptoe, brings him a glass of tea, he is sitting in an easy chair as before with his eyes closed, absorbed in his lyrics. He does not stir, drums lightly on his forehead with two fingers, and pretends he is not aware of his wife's presence. His face wears an expression of injured innocence.

Like a girl who has been presented with a costly necklace, he spends a long time posing to himself before he writes the title of the song. He presses his temples, he wriggles, draws his legs up under his chair as though he were in pain, or half closes his eyes like a cat on the sofa. At last, not without hesitation, he stretches out his hand toward the paper, and with an expression as though he were signing a death warrant, writes the title.

"Can I have some water?" he hears his daughter's voice.

"Hush, Haley!" says his wife. "Daddy's writing! Hush!"

Eminem writes very, very quickly, without corrections or pauses. He scarcely has time to turn over the pages. The busts and portraits of celebrated rappers look at his swiftly racing pencil and, keeping stock-still, seem to be thinking: You really are at it!

"Sh!" squeaks the pencil.

"Sh!" whisper the rappers, when his knee jolts the table and they are set trembling.

All at once Eminem draws himself up, lays down his pencil, and listens. He hears an even, monotonous whispering. It is Dr. Dre, who furnishes him with many of his beats. He has come into the house and is speaking softly to Kim.

"Dre, come on!" cries Eminem. "Couldn't you please speak more quietly? You're preventing me from writing!"

"Very sorry," Dr. Dre answers. "But maybe you should close the door if you don't want to hear people."

"But then how would you hear me?"

"That wouldn't be important," Dr. Dre says. "You wouldn't need to speak to me. You wouldn't even know I was here."

"Why are you here?" Eminem says. "It's almost midnight."

"I wanted to see if I left a key-chain drive here yesterday. It has some work I was doing for Snoop."

After finishing two more songs, Eminem stretches and looks at his watch.

"Three o'clock already," he moans. "Other people are asleep while I must work!"

Shattered and exhausted, he goes, with his head on one side, to the bedroom to wake his wife, and says in a languid voice:

"Kim, I need some more tea! I feel weak."

He writes till four o'clock and would readily have written till six if his subject had not been exhausted. Making the most of himself and the inanimate objects around him, far from any critical eye, tyrannizing and domineering over the little anthill that fate has put in his power are the honey and the salt of his existence. And how different is this despot here at home from the humble, meek man he secretly believes himself to be.

"I am so exhausted that I am afraid I won't sleep," he says as he gets into bed. "My work exhausts the soul even more than the body. I had better take a pill. God knows, I'd like to one day be done with this. To write to make a release date that someone else has set? It is awful."

He sleeps till twelve or one o'clock in the day, sleeps a sound, healthy sleep. How well he would sleep, what dreams he would have, if he could somehow entrust others with the writing of his albums!

"He has been writing all night," whispers his wife with a scared expression on her face. "Shh!"

No one dares to speak or move or make a sound. His sleep is something sacred, and the culprit who offends against it will pay dearly for his fault.

"Hush!" floats across the house. "Hush!"

An Enigmatic Nature

ON A GRAY LEATHER SEAT IN THE FIRST-CLASS PORTION OF AN airplane, Oprah Winfrey sits half reclining. She has a blanket spread over her legs, her overhead air turned on, and a book in her lap that she opens now and again, pages through, and sets down. She is greatly agitated.

On the seat next to her is a budding young author who has published one novel about a young boy growing up in the nineteen-eighties and is beginning work on a more ambitious project about the life and death of an American city. He is gazing into Oprah's face, gazing intently, with the eyes of a connoisseur. He is watching, studying, catching every shade of this exceptional, enigmatic nature. He understands it, he fathoms it. Her soul, her whole psychology, lies open before him.

"I know who you are," he says. "But I don't mean it the way you think." He has been drinking, and he touches her elbow. "Everyone sees a certain thing about you, but I see a sensitive, responsive soul. You show it, but you can't really show it. The struggle is terrific, titanic. But do not lose heart. You will be triumphant!"

"Write about me," says Oprah with a mournful smile. "My life has been so full, so varied, so checkered, so perfect. I should be happy. I tell everyone to be that way. I teach everyone to be that way. And yet I suffer. Reveal that soul to the world. Reveal that hapless soul. You are a psychologist. We've only been on the plane an hour together, and you have already fathomed my heart."

"Tell me what you mean," the author says.

"Listen. It starts in Mississippi. My parents were never married. My father had a good heart and was not without intelligence, but the way things were then . . . he worked in a coal mine, cut hair . . . I do not blame my father. My mother—but why say more? She left to move north and find work, and I stayed behind with my grandmother. I got beaten. I got educated. I went to school dressed in burlap. It was awful! The challenges! The sense of hopelessness! And the agonies of losing faith in life, in oneself! You are an author. You know us women. You will understand. I have always had an intense nature. I looked for happiness—and what happiness! I longed to set my soul free. Yes. In that I saw my happiness!"

"That's exactly right," murmurs the author, touching her arm just above the elbow. "I have heard this told, or read about it, but it is so different to hear it directly from you."

"Oh, I longed for glory, renown, success, like every—why affect modesty?—every nature above the commonplace. I yearned for something extraordinary, above the common lot of woman! And then, I was seized by the radio business, and then by television. It is not too much to say that the opportunity took me violently. I sacrificed myself to that life as much as any woman ever sacrifices herself to a husband or a lover. You must see that! I could do nothing else. I began to see some money, to make a name for myself. There were moments—terrible moments—but I was kept afloat by the thought that one day I would lift myself even higher, that I would control the process that had controlled me!"

Oprah returns to her book, turns a few more pages. Her face has fallen into sadness. She goes on:

"There was a point where I sensed I might be done with it all. I was hosting *Dialing for Dollars* in Baltimore. Things were coming to a close. I thought I'd have my freedom. That was the moment I should have left definitively. But then came Chicago, and my morning show. It started as a half hour. It went to an hour. It went into syndication. It went national. It went worldwide. What could have been my freedom was my captivity once again. Don't misunderstand me. It is a wonderful kind of captivity, but it is also wretched. The things I have seen, the things I have not let myself feel. How ignoble, repulsive, and senseless life is. I dated John Tesh. I have recently been thinking about freedom again, but again there is an obstacle in my path, and again I feel that my happiness is far, far away. It is anguish—if only you knew."

"What stands in your way? Tell me! What is it?"

"It is success. It is fame. It is the need to do good for others, to offer the full power of my assistance. This cycle never ends. It cannot end, because it is the correct thing for me to do, and yet there are times when I cannot bear it any longer."

The book conceals her face. The author props his chin on his fist and ponders with the air of a professional. The engines of the plane thrum on either side of them as the glow of the setting sun fills the window.

Not Wanted

Between six and seven o'clock on a July evening, a crowd of summer visitors—mostly fathers of families—burdened with suitcases and shoulder bags, was trailing along from the ferry-boat dock. They all looked exhausted, hungry, and ill-humored, as though the sun were not shining and the sand was not white for them.

Trudging along among the others was Alec Baldwin, a broad, round-shouldered man in a cotton coat and khaki pants. He was perspiring and gloomy.

"Do you come out to your holiday home every weekend?" said a man in salmon-colored pants, addressing him.

"Not every weekend," Alec Baldwin answered sullenly. "My wife and daughter are staying all summer, and I come here when I can. I don't have time to come every week; besides, it is expensive."

"You're right there; it is expensive," sighed the man with the salmon pants. "You coming up from the city? They used to run a boat directly from there to here, but when they did, they charged through the nose for everything. Chips were like six dollars. Now you have to go by train first, then by boat, and that has its own set of costs. Or you can drive the whole way, but to feel better about driving, you'll want to rent a nice car, or to take your own car, but either way it just sits in the lot all week. It's all small potatoes not worth worrying about, but over the course of the summer it adds up. Of course, to be in the lap of Nature is worth any money—I don't dispute it, perfect peace and all the rest of it; but of course, on my salary, every dollar has to be considered. If I waste a penny I lie awake all night. You know what? I'm sorry, I haven't asked your name. I receive a salary of almost a hundred thousand dollars, I smoke cheap cigars, and still I don't have a dollar to spare to buy myself the whiskey I like."

"It's altogether abominable," said Alec Baldwin after a brief silence. "I maintain that summer holidays are the invention of the devil and of woman. The devil was motivated by malice, woman by excessive frivolity. Mercy on us, it is not life at all; it is hard labor, it is hell! It's hot and stifling, you can hardly breathe, and you wander about like a lost soul and find no refuge. Back in the city there is no food and no drink at home. Everything has been carried off to the summer place: you eat what you can get; you go without your coffee because there is no coffeemaker; you can't even take the shower you want because the shampoo and the washcloth is gone; and then when you come down here into the lap of Nature you have to slog through the heat and the humidity! Unbelievable. Are you married?"

"Yes, three children," sighed Salmon Pants.

"It's horrible. It's a wonder we are still alive."

At last the bus came. Alec Baldwin said good-bye to Salmon Pants and boarded. In twenty minutes he was standing outside his house. He could hear nothing but the distant ocean and the prayer for help of a fly destined for the dinner of a spider. He went inside. The windows were hung with sheer curtains, through which faded flowers showed red. On an unpainted wooden wall there was a large fuzzy caterpillar. There was not a soul in the hallway, the kitchen, or the dining room. In an upstairs room that had no name, Alec Baldwin found his daughter, Ireland, a little girl of ten. Ireland was sitting at the table and breathing loudly with her lower lip stuck out. She was engaged in cutting up the jack of diamonds from a deck of cards.

"Oh, it's you, Dad!" she said, without turning round. "You're here."

"I am. And where is Mom?"

"Mom? She went over to Mary and Ted's. They're organizing some kind of show. A benefit. It's this weekend. She says I can go. Will you go with us?"

"When is she coming back?"

"She's supposed to be back pretty soon."

"And where is Jenny? Isn't she supposed to be your babysitter?"

"Mom took Jenny with her to help her carry some things back. Dad, why is it that when mosquitoes bite you they don't get too fat to fly?"

"I don't know. They must be strong fliers. So there is no one in the house, then?"

"Just me."

Alec Baldwin sat down in an chair and for a moment gazed blankly at the window.

"Who is going to get our dinner?" he asked.

"There isn't dinner. Mom thought you were coming tomorrow. She is going to have dinner over there, I think."

"Oh, thank you very much; and you, what did you have to eat for lunch?"

"I had some chocolate milk and a sandwich. And chips. Dad, do mosquitoes mix our blood with their own?"

Alec Baldwin suddenly felt as though something heavy was rolling down on his liver and beginning to gnaw in it. He felt so angry, so pained, and so bitter, that he was choking and tremulous; he wanted to jump up, to bang something on the floor, and to burst into loud shouting; but then he remembered that his doctor had absolutely forbidden him all excitement, so he got up, and making an effort to control himself, began whistling.

"Dad, does an actor ever forget who he is for real?" he heard Ireland's voice.

"Oh, don't bother me with stupid questions!" said Alec Baldwin, getting angry. "Kids stick to you like a leaf in the bath! Here you are, ten years old, and just as silly as you were three years ago. Why are you ruining those cards? What if I want to play solitaire?"

"These cards aren't yours," said Ireland, turning around. "Mom gave them to me."

"You are telling lies, you are telling lies!" said Alec Baldwin, growing more and more irritated. "You are always lying! What is your problem?"

Ireland leapt up, and moving her face in close, stared at her father. Her big eyes first began blinking, then were dimmed with moisture, and the girl's face began working.

"But why are you yelling?" said Ireland. "Why are you mean to me? I am not doing anything wrong. I was just sitting here and you're mad. Why are you yelling?"

The girl spoke with conviction, and cried so bitterly that Alec Baldwin felt conscience-stricken.

Yes, really, why am I doing this? he thought. "Come on," he said, touching the girl on the shoulder. "I am sorry, Ireland. Forgive me. You are my good girl. I love you."

Ireland wiped her eyes with his sleeve, sat down, with a sigh, in the same place and began cutting out the queen. Alec Baldwin went off to his own room. He stretched himself on the sofa, and putting his hands behind his head, sank into thought. The girl's tears had softened his anger, and by degrees the oppression on his conscience grew less. He felt nothing but exhaustion and hunger.

"Dad," he heard on the other side of the door, "can I show you my collection of insects?"

"Yes, show me."

Ireland came into the study and handed her father a long green box. Before raising it to his ear Alec Baldwin could hear a despairing buzz and the scratching of claws on the sides of the box. Opening the lid, he saw a number of butterflies, beetles, grasshoppers, and flies fastened to the bottom of the box with pins. All except two or three butterflies were still alive and moving.

"The grasshopper is still alive!" said Ireland in surprise. "I caught him yesterday morning, and he is still alive!"

"Who taught you to pin them this way?"

"Jenny did."

"Jenny ought to be pinned down like that herself!" said Alec Baldwin. "Take them away! It's shameful to torture animals. And it's strange for a girl to do this, at any rate. Cards, insects: it's almost as if you have your own personality."

How horribly she is being brought up! he thought as Ireland went out.

Alec Baldwin forgot his exhaustion and hunger, and thought of nothing but his girl's future. Meanwhile, outside the light was gradually fading. . . . He could hear the summer visitors trooping back from the beach. Someone was stopping near the open dining-room window and shouting: "Do you want any mushrooms?" And getting no answer, shuffled on with bare feet. At last, when the dusk was so thick that the outlines of the flowers behind the muslin curtain were lost, and whiffs of the freshness of evening were coming in at the window, he heard noises up the path, footsteps crunching the gravel, talk and laughter.

"Mom!" shrieked Ireland.

Alec Baldwin peeped out of his study and saw his wife, Kim, healthy and rosy as ever; with her he saw Mary Steenburgen, a tall woman with dark hair and a long thin neck; and two younger men: one a lanky fellow with a manicured look and a goatee; the other a short stubby man with a shaven face and a bluish crooked chin. Jenny was trailing behind them, carrying a box.

"Jenny, can you mix up some drinks?" said Kim. "It looks like Alec has finally shown up. Alec, where are you?" she said, running into the study breathlessly. "So you've come. I'm glad. I brought some people over from Mary and Ted's. Come, I'll introduce you."

"Just tell me who they are. They look vaguely familiar."

"The tall one is Will.i.am. He sings and produces music. The other one, the shorter man, is Tracy Morgan, who is an actor and a comedian. We're going to use them both for the benefit this weekend. Oh, how tired I am! We were singing while Ted played the piano."

"Why did you bring them here?" asked Alec Baldwin.

"I couldn't help it. After dinner I want Will to go through his songs. Oh, yes, I almost forgot! Will you send Jenny to get some thin-sliced prosciutto, cheese, fruit, and something else? Will.i.am and Tracy Morgan might stay to eat. Oh, how tired I am!"

"I don't have money for Jenny."

"Sure you do."

Half an hour later Jenny was sent to the store. Alec Baldwin, after drinking a glass of red wine and eating a whole loaf of bread, went to his bedroom and lay down on the bed, while Kim and her visitors, with much noise and laughter, set to work to rehearse their songs. For a long time Alec Baldwin heard Tracy Morgan's voice and some kind of drumming he supposed came from Will.i.am. The rehearsal was followed by a long conversation, interrupted by Mary's shrill laughter.

Then followed more singing, and then the clattering of crockery. Through his drowsiness Alec Baldwin heard them persuading Patton Oswalt to perform scenes from movies he had been in, and heard him, after affecting to refuse, begin to recite. He hissed, beat himself on the chest, wept, laughed in a husky bass. Alec Baldwin scowled and hid his head under the quilt.

"It's a long way for you to go, and it's dark," he heard Kim's voice an hour later. "Why shouldn't you stay the night here? Will.i.am can sleep here on the sofa, and you, Tracy Morgan, in Ireland's bed. I can put her in Alec's study. Do stay, really!"

At last, when the clock was striking midnight, all was hushed, the bedroom door opened, and Kim appeared.

"Alec, are you asleep?" she whispered.

"No; why?"

"Go into your study and lie on the sofa. I am going to let Mary sleep in here with me. I'd put her in the study, but she is afraid to sleep alone. Come on."

Alec Baldwin got up, threw on his robe, and taking his pillow, crept wearily to the study. Feeling his way to his sofa, he reached for a lamp, turned it on, and saw Ireland lying on the sofa. The girl was not asleep. She was staring at the ceiling with wide eyes:

"Dad, why don't mosquitoes sleep at night?" she asked.

"Because we're not wanted. We have nowhere to even rest for a minute."

"And why does Mary have dark hair now when her hair used to be light?"

"That's enough questions for today. Maybe forever."

After a moment's thought Alec Baldwin dressed and went outside to walk along the road. He looked at the gray sky, at the motionless clouds, heard the lazy call of a seabird, and began dreaming of the next day, when he could send Kim off to practice for the benefit, and Ireland with her, and he could tumble into bed. After a little while he saw a car parked on the shoulder. It was running and the lights were on. A man was sitting in the driver's seat.

Maybe it's the police, thought Alec Baldwin. They patrolled sometimes late at night. He waved, as he was accustomed to doing with police. But as he drew closer, he recognized the man from the ferryboat, the one with the salmon pants.

"Hey," Alec Baldwin said, tapping on the window. The man rolled it down. "You live around here?"

"Just up the road," sighed Salmon Pants.

"Why aren't you there now?"

"My wife's mother came in late this evening. She brought our nieces with her. Great girls, but when you get three generations of related women together, well, let's just say that it was time for me to go for a little drive. Are you enjoying your evening?"

"Yes," said Alec Baldwin. "It's hard to imagine anything quite so pleasant. Do you know if there is any kind of restaurant open this late on this part of the island?"

Salmon Pants raised his eyes to heaven and meditated profoundly.

JOY

I T WAS TWELVE O'CLOCK AT NIGHT.

Kim Kardashian, with excited face and ruffled hair, flew into her family's house and hurriedly ran through all the rooms. Her parents had already gone to bed. Her sisters were awake, trying on lingerie. Her stepbrother was looking at himself in the mirror.

"Where have you come from?" her sister Khloe cried in amazement. "What is the matter with you?"

"Oh, don't ask! I never expected it; no, I never expected it! It's positively incredible!"

Kim laughed and sank into an armchair, so overcome by happiness that she could not stand on her legs.

"It's incredible! You can't imagine! Look!"

Her other sister, Kourtney, threw a quilt round her and went in to fetch their stepbrother Brody. He came into the room, holding a hand mirror. Within a moment Kim's parents were in the room as well.

"What's the matter?" her mother said. "You don't look like yourself!"

"It's because I am so happy. The whole world knows me! The whole world! Until now only you knew that there was a girl called Kim Kardashian, and now the whole world knows it! Mama! Thank heavens!"

Kim jumped up, ran up and down all the rooms, and then sat down again.

"What has happened? Tell us sensibly!"

"You live like wild beasts, you don't watch very much television and take no notice of what's online, and there's so much that is interesting there. If anything happens it's all known at once, nothing is hidden! How happy I am! Oh, Lord! You know it's only celebrated people whose names are published online, and now they have gone and published mine!"

"What do you mean? Where?"

Kim's stepfather, Bruce Jenner, turned pale. Her mother crossed herself. Brody looked at her and then looked back into the hand mirror.

"Yes! My name has been published! Now all the world knows of me! Bookmark that page and print it out in memory! We will read it sometimes! Look!"

Kim went to the computer, tapped a series of keys, and then pointed to a paragraph on the screen.

"Read it!" she said to Bruce Jenner.

He put on his glasses.

"Read it!"

Kim's mother crossed herself again. Bruce Jenner cleared his throat and began to read: "'We will all be hearing more of Kim Kardashian soon . . .'"

"You see, you see! Go on!"

"'. . . since an intimate video starring Kardashian and her ex-boyfriend has been confirmed . . .'"

"That's me and Ray J . . . it's all described exactly! Go on! Listen!"

"'. . . and will be released later this month. The tape, which Vivid reportedly acquired for one million dollars, includes more than thirty minutes of explicit sexual activity . . .'"

"Go on! Read the rest!"

"'It was filmed a few years ago, when Kardashian and her boyfriend, an R&B singer named Ray J . . .'"

"I told you. Ray J! But keep reading. There's more about me."

"'Initially, Kardashian tried to block the release of the tape, but at length came to an agreement with the distribution company.'"

"That's right. I'm being distributed. You have read it now? Good! So you see. It's all over the Internet, which means it's all over the world! Give it here!"

Kim closed the window and turned away from the computer.

"I have to go around the neighborhood and show this to a bunch of other people . . . the Gastineaus . . . the Hiltons. . . . Must run! Good-bye!"

Kim put on her hat and, joyful and triumphant, ran into the street.

At the Barber's

It is not yet seven o'clock, but the barbershop is already open. The barber himself, an unwashed, greasy youth of twenty-three, is busy clearing up; there is really nothing to be cleared away, but he is perspiring with his exertions. In one place he polishes with a rag, in another he scrapes with his finger or catches a bug and brushes it off the wall.

The barber's shop is small, narrow, and unclean. The walls are hung with faded paper decorated with cowboy hats and tin stars. Between the two dingy, perspiring windows there is a thin, creaking, rickety door, and above it a bell that trembles and gives a sickly ring of itself without provocation. Glance into the mirror that hangs on one of the walls, and it distorts your face in all directions in the most merciless way! The shaving and haircutting is done before this mirror. On the little table, as greasy and unwashed as the barber himself, there is everything: combs, scissors, razors, wax for the moustache, powder, watered-down cologne. The whole shop is not worth more than five hundred dollars.

There is a squeaking sound from the bell and an older man in a tanned sheepskin coat and high felt overboots walks into the shop. His head and neck are wrapped in a black scarf.

This is Billy Ray Cyrus, who patronizes the shop as a result of his friendship with the barber's father.

"Good morning, son!" he says to the barber, who is absorbed in tidying up.

They shake hands. Billy Ray Cyrus drags his scarf off his head and sits down.

"What a long way it is!" he says, sighing and clearing his throat. "It's no joke! From my house to here is almost two hours."

"How are you?"

"Feeling poorly. I've had a fever."

"A fever!"

"Yes, I have been in bed almost a week; I thought I might die. Then I had some complication, some vitamin deficiency, and a clump of my hair came out. Now my hair's coming out. The doctor says I must be shaved. He says the hair will grow again strong. So that's why I'm here. Better you than a stranger. You'll do it better and won't make me feel strange about it. Plus, it's free. Except for the two-hour drive."

"Of course. With pleasure. Please sit down."

With a scrape of his foot the barber indicates a chair. Billy Ray Cyrus sits down and looks at himself in the glass and is apparently pleased with his reflection: the looking glass displays a face awry, with thin lips, a sharp nose, and eyes set high, almost in the forehead. The barber puts round his client's shoulders a white sheet with yellow spots on it, and begins snipping with the scissors.

"I'll shave you clean to the skin!" he says.

"Do it. I want to look like a bomb. The doctor says it'll grow back thicker."

"How's Jackie Chan? The two of you are working on a movie together, right?"

"Yes. He sprained his ankle earlier this month."

"His ankle? Too bad, though he must be used to that kind of thing. Hold your ear."

"I am holding it. . . . Don't cut me. Ouch! You are pulling my hair."

"That doesn't matter. We can't help that in our work. And how is your daughter Miley?"

"Good, good. She was single for a bit, but then she got engaged. She's going to have a big wedding. You should come."

The scissors cease snipping. The young barber drops his hands and asks in a fright:

"Who is betrothed?"

"Miley."

"How's that? To whom?"

"To some guy named Steve. Steve Adams? He has a few stores near Sacramento. She swore off actors and celebrities, you know, because she doesn't really need money. We were worried she wouldn't find someone she could be herself around, but this guy seems great. We are all delighted. The wedding will be in two weeks. You should come; we will have a good time."

"This is impossible," says the barber, pale, astonished, and shrugging his shoulders. "It's . . . it's utterly impossible. Why, Miley . . . why I . . . why, I cherished sentiments for her, I had intentions. We spoke at length last summer about her decision to be done with actors. I thought she had a sense of me, of how I could make her happy. How could this be?"

"Why, we just went and betrothed her. He's a good fellow."

Cold drops of perspiration come on the face of the barber. He puts the scissors down on the table and begins rubbing his nose with his fist.

"I had intentions," he says. "It's impossible. I am in love with her and have just recently sent her a letter offering my heart. I have always respected you as though you were my father. I always cut your hair for nothing. When my father died you came in here and took some paintings off the walls and gave me nothing for them. Do you remember?"

"Remember! Of course I do. I love you like a son. But do you think you are a pair with Miley? It seems unlikely. You have no money and no standing. You are a barber."

"And is Steve Adams rich?"

"Steve Adams is in sporting goods. He's a little older than you are. He owns his house. Look. It's no good talking about it. The thing's done. You must look out for another bride. The world is not so small. Come, cut away. Why are you stopping?"

The barber remains motionless for a while. When he moves, it is to take a handkerchief out of his pocket. He begins to cry into it.

"What is it?" Billy Ray Cyrus comforts him. "Stop it. Damn it, you're crying like an old woman! Finish my head and then cry. Don't put down the clippers!"

The barber takes up the clippers, stares vacantly at them for a minute, then drops them again on the table. His hands are shaking.

"I can't," he says. "I can't do it just now. I haven't the strength! I am a miserable man! And she is miserable, I'm sure, with Steve Adams! Last summer we pledged our love to one another. We gave each other our promise. Now we have been separated by unkind people without any pity. Go away! I can't bear the sight of you."

Billy Ray Cyrus comes to his feet. "So I'll come tomorrow. You'll finish up then."

"Right."

"Get calm, and I'll come by early in the morning."

Billy Ray Cyrus has half his head shaven to the skin and looks like a convict. It is awkward to be left with a head like that, but there is no help for it. He wraps his head in the scarf and walks out of the barbershop. Left alone, the barber sits down and goes on quietly weeping.

Early the next morning the bell squeaks and Billy Ray Cyrus comes into the shop.

"What do you want?" the barber asks him coldly.

"Finish cutting my hair. There is half the head left to do."

"Kindly give me the money in advance. I won't cut it for nothing."

Without saying a word, Billy Ray Cyrus goes out, and to this day his hair is long on one side of the head and short on the other. He regards it as extravagance to pay for having his hair cut and is waiting for the hair to grow of itself on the shaven side.

He danced at the wedding in that condition.

CHORISTERS

D URING THE SHOW'S EIGHTH SEASON, THE PRODUCER, WHO HAD received a call from Dublin, set the news going that Bono would soon be arriving. When he would arrive—there was no saying.

"He moves in mysterious ways," said Paula Abdul, who was wearing a lilac minidress. "But when he does come the place will be even crazier than it is now. It's Bono. He really draws a crowd. So let's make a special effort to get them ready. I want him to be proud of them, and of us. "

"Don't worry about me," said Simon Cowell, frowning.

"I won't," Paula Abdul said. "I'll round up the others so we can get going."

Simon Cowell was the main judge of *American Idol*, a competition where young singers attempted to earn a record contract and international fame. He was paid handsomely by the show. Simon Cowell was a man of confident deportment. His dark hair and cleft chin made him look like an important man. It was strange to see him, so dignified and imposing, turn shy in the presence of the established stars who visited the show as guest judges, and on one occasion refuse to come out of his dressing room because he could not face Elton John. Grandeur was more in keeping with his figure than humility.

On account of the rumors of Bono's visit, the nine singers remaining in the competition took a number of extra practices.

Practice was held at a small building near the Kodak Theatre, and this is how it was conducted. Before the practice Randy Jackson and Paula Abdul talked to the young singers encouragingly and regaled them with stories about the music business. When Simon Cowell arrived, he came quickly to the front of the room and issued a series of sharp claps. The young men who were still in the competition, who had been sitting on the floor listening to the day's songs, took out their earphones and stood slowly. The young women, who had been smoking just outside the doorway, came tramping in. They all took their places. Simon Cowell drew himself up, made a sign to enforce silence, and began issuing instructions.

"You cannot forget the lyrics. I hope you have studied.

"If you do not act like you belong here, you will not be here much longer.

"Song choice is vitally important in this competition."

All this counsel had been given the week before and the week before that, repeated a thousand times and thoroughly digested, and it was gone through simply as a formality. The singers began to work through their songs. The judges watched the first performers, shook their heads, occasionally nodded. It was all as it was the day before; there was nothing new. The singers who were waiting their turn began to lose interest. There was some coughing and fidgeting. Earphones went back in ears. Simon Cowell called for a break, and went off to the side to speak to Randy Jackson. After a few minutes he stood back up and called the entire group to attention.

"There will be a slight change of plans. You will all be setting aside whatever song you have selected. Instead, you'll sing a U2 song. There are lyric sheets in the corner." A woman appeared in the corner of the room and shook a sheaf of papers. "Go pick one and let's get started. You don't need to get the words exactly right. These are mostly songs that you know. Just give them your best try. Be spontaneous."

The first singer, a woman, tried her hand at "All I Want Is You." When she reached the chorus, an expression of benevolence and amiability overspread Simon Cowell's face, as though he were dreaming of a lovely meal.

"Next singer!"

It was a man, attempting "Where the Streets Have No Name," and he was not as successful: Simon Cowell's face expressed alarm and even horror.

But then came "With or Without You" and then "One," both sung so well that the other singers stopped fidgeting and gave them their full attention. The production assistants, who were always busy copying lyrics and jotting down notes, abandoned their work and fell to watching the performances. After a confused version of "Angel of Harlem" and an uneven "I Still Haven't Found What I'm Looking For," Simon Cowell wiped the sweat off his brow and went up to Randy Jackson in excitement.

"It puzzles me," he said, shrugging his shoulders. "Why is it that young singers are up one minute and down the next? You can't tell whether they are finally grasping a song or if that understanding is a put-on, like so much else about them. Were you choking, or what?" he asked, addressing one of the female singers, a tall brunette with hair so straight it looked ironed.

"Why?"

"Because of your voice. It rattles like a pan under a car. What is Bono going to think when you take his song and treat it like an advertising jingle? I would be surprised if you are here a week from now."

"You look a little tired," said Paula Abdul.

"Are you still treating this competition like a big party? Maybe you should spend less time trying to attract the attention of the boys. If that's what you want to do, you can do that on any street corner in the town you'll be returning to soon enough."

"Don't get so worked up," said Randy Jackson. "I'll talk to her."

Randy Jackson took the girl off to one side. "Just try to con-
centrate. It's a big week coming up. You've heard the rumors about
Bono. This is important for all of us."

The brunette scratched her neck and looked sideways toward
the window, as though the words did not apply to her.

The singers went on in this impromptu fashion for the rest of
the afternoon, trying their hands at other songs: "Bullet the Blue
Sky," "Stuck in a Moment You Can't Get Out Of," even "Numb."
For the most part they sang smoothly and with feeling, even the
tall brunette.

"You know, Randy," Simon Cowell said. "Maybe we should
change things entirely, have them perform an album in full, one
singing the first song, the next the second, and so on."

"No, no. Let them sing from whatever album they want. If it
seems too calculated, it may feel strange to all of us."

The group took another break. There was again a great blow-
ing of noses, coughing, turning over of pages, and fiddling with
phones. The most difficult part of the practice was next: "group
sing," in which the contestants performed one song together, in
rounds. Simon Cowell had put two choices before the group,
"Beautiful Day" and "Stay (Faraway, So Close)." Whichever the
group learned best would be sung before Bono. During "group
sing" Simon Cowell's face reflected a high pitch of enthusiasm.
Expressions of benevolence were continually alternating with expressions of alarm.

"Don't do the chorus that way!" he muttered. "Try to start at the same volume that the singer before you ended. Make sure you understand the lyrics, at least a little bit."

His words were launched at the young men and women like missiles. His eyes were closed more than they were open. On one occasion, carried away by his feelings, he raised a hand as if he were going to strike the singer closest to him, though he did not bring it down. But the contestants were not moved to tears or to anger: they realized the full gravity of their task.

After "group sing" came a minute of silence. Simon Cowell, red, perspiring, and exhausted, leaned against the wall near the door, and then turned upon the contestants tired but triumphant eyes. He let the silence spread to fill the room. It was a form of approval. Then, to his immense annoyance, the door opened and Kara DioGuardi came into the practice room. She was the fourth judge, a new addition to the show, and as she had not yet learned to fit in with the other three, she often arrived late to practice. She had a contemptuous grin on her face.

"Go ahead," she said. "Get back to group sing. I was outside listening, and I don't think Bono's going to like it."

Randy Jackson looked around nervously and twiddled his fingers.

"Come on," he muttered. "Don't start."

After "group sing" the contestants reflected on the songs they had chosen, and what they meant, and whether or not they would keep that same selection for the night of the live performance. Then practice was over. The contestants went to eat and to nap, and they reassembled in the evening for another practice. And so it went that day and the next.

On the third day, the show's producer received a note that seemed to confirm Bono's arrival. The lights in the Kodak Theatre were turned off and on, the sound system checked, and the full band began to rehearse. Simon Cowell couldn't sleep well, though he couldn't say whether it was from delight or alarm. Kara Dio-Guardi went on grinning.

The day before the live show, Randy Jackson burst into Simon Cowell's dressing room. His hands shook and his eyes looked faded.

"I was just talking to the producers," he said, stammering. "They are still negotiating with Bono. I asked them if he's going to sit in and judge the final rehearsals along with the broadcast, and they said he might just send a videotaped message. A videotaped message?"

Simon Cowell turned crimson. He would rather have spent two hours listening to Paula Abdul speak than have heard those words. He did not sleep all night. He was not so much mortified at the waste of his efforts as at the fact that Kara DioGuardi would give him no peace now with her mockery. Kara DioGuardi was delighted at his discomfiture.

The next morning, all through rehearsal, she was casting significant glances down the table at Simon Cowell. When they took a break she put her hand over her microphone and said:

"No wonder Bono has better things to do."

After the rehearsal, Simon Cowell went home, crushed and ill with chagrin. He told himself several times that he could not continue on like this. "I must leave the show," he said. "I must leave the show." He made a list of possible replacements for himself and tore it up. Again he could not sleep, and he went down to the lobby. The elevator opened to show Kara DioGuardi. Her face was red.

"Hold on, Simon," she said. "Wait a minute. Don't be mad. You are not the only one. I am in this too. When the producers were on the phone with Bono trying to decide if he'd come or send a taped message, he called me Carrie. They corrected him, and you know what he said? 'You know which one I mean,' he said. 'That bloody loose bit.' A big star, and that's how he treats me? Let me buy you a drink."

And the enemies went to the bar arm in arm.

A Classical Student

BEFORE SETTING OFF FOR HER AUDITION, LINDSAY LOHAN KISSED all the movie posters. Her stomach felt as though it were upside down; there was a chill at her heart, while the heart itself throbbed and stood still with terror before the unknown. What would she get that day? An offer? A callback? Six times she went to her mother for her blessing, and, as she went out, asked her sister to pray for her. On the way to the audition she gave a homeless man five dollars, in the hope that the five dollars would atone for her ignorance, and that she would not forget her lines or what her character was feeling.

She came back from the audition late, between four and five. She came in and noiselessly lay down on her bed. Her freckled face was pale and looked even thinner than usual. There were dark lines beneath her eyes.

"Well, how was it? What did they think? Was the director there?" asked her mother, Dina, going to her bedside.

Lindsay blinked, twisted her mouth, and burst into tears. Her mother turned pale, let her mouth fall open, and clasped her hands. The magazine she was reading dropped to the floor.

"What are you crying for? You've failed, then?" her mother asked.

"They said it was fine and that they'd be in touch, but I know what that means."

"I knew this would happen! I had a dream last night," said her mother. "God! How is it you can't get real roles? What is the reason? What kind of movie was this again?"

"A teen comedy based on Shakespeare. I knew the lines perfect, but when they asked me to explain them, I froze up. I was reading from the scene where I come out of my bedroom in the middle of the night, and I don't feel well because of this murder I did, I mean my character of course, and there's a doctor standing nearby. I thought I would try something different, and go to the doctor for help—not the real doctor, but the doctor in the play—but it turns out my character is sleepwalking and I'm not supposed to know, she's not supposed to know, that the doctor is even there. I think they thought I didn't understand. I am miserable. I was working on this all week."

"It's not you who should be miserable, but me. I'm miserable. I've finally had enough. This is the last straw. I have been taking you to auditions since you were a little girl. I've broken my back for you. This is a role that should be a breeze to get. Why can't you just try harder?"

"I . . . I am trying as hard as I know. I'm up until three or four every night practicing. You've seen it yourself."

"I prayed to God to take me, but He leaves me here to suffer from you. Other people have children like everyone else. I get pleasure and comfort from your sister but none from you. I'd beat you, but where am I to find the strength? Mother of God, where am I to find the strength?"

The mother hid her face in the folds of her blouse and broke into sobs. Lindsay wriggled with anguish and pressed her forehead against the wall. Lindsay's sister Ali came into the room.

"So that's how it is. Just what I expected," Ali said, at once guessing what was wrong, turning pale. "I've been depressed all afternoon, while you were out at the audition. There's trouble coming, I thought, and here it is."

"No comfort! Where can I find the strength? God damn it."

"Why are you swearing at her?" cried the sister, turning upon the mother. "It's not her fault! It's your fault! You are to blame! Why did you start taking her to auditions? You want to be rich? You're rich. It's not like you're going to turn into an aristocrat. You should have sent her into business, or made her work for a real company. Sure, she had some success, but she'll drop out of view for long stretches in years to come. And you are wearing yourself out, and wearing her out! She is thin. She coughs constantly. Just look at her!"

"No, Ali, no! I haven't beaten her enough! She ought to have been beaten, that's what it is!" The mother shook her fist at her daughters. "You want a flogging, but I haven't the strength. They told me years ago when she was little, 'Whip her, whip her!' I didn't heed them, and now I am suffering for it. You wait a bit! I'll flay you! Wait a bit."

Dina shook her fist, and went weeping into the other room, where her houseguest was sitting. The houseguest, Jesse James, was sitting at a table, reading Shakespeare, of all things. Jesse James was a man of intelligence and education, though he sometimes concealed it. When he was alone, he spoke through his nose, and washed with a soap that made everyone in the house sneeze. He was forever on the lookout for women of refined education.

"My good friend," began Dina, dissolving into tears. "If you would have the generosity to thrash my girl for me. Do me the favor! She failed another audition, that one! Would you believe it? A failure, again. I can't punish her, through the weakness of my ill health. Thrash her for me, if you would be so considerate! Have regard for a sick woman!"

Jesse James frowned and heaved a deep sigh. He thought a little, drummed on the table with his fingers, and, sighing once more, went to Lindsay.

"You are being encouraged," he began, "being given a great opportunity, you revolting young person! Why have you done this?"

He talked for a long time, made a speech. He alluded to science, to light, to darkness, to democracy.

When he had finished his speech, he took off his belt and took Lindsay by the hand.

"It's the only way to deal with you," he said. Lindsay knelt down submissively and thrust her head between the houseguest's knees. Her prominent pink ears moved up and down against his new trousers, which had brown stripes on the outer seams.

Lindsay did not utter a single sound. At the family council in the evening, it was decided to send her into business.

TERROR

MICHAEL DOUGLAS ACTED FOR YEARS, BUT AT SOME POINT IN his sixties retired to run a series of coffee shops: not just to own them and to oversee them, but to work in them. This endeavor was fairly successful, and yet it always seemed to me that he was not in his proper place, and that he would do well to go back to Hollywood. When tired, fingers stained, smelling of coffee, he waved to me from behind the counter, and then later on the street seemed almost entranced by his own fatigue, I saw him not as a businessman or a barista, but only as a worried and exhausted man, and it was clear to me that he did not really care for coffee, but that all he wanted was for the day to be over.

I liked to be with him, and I used to stay in the shops as long as I could. I liked the big one on Maple Street, and the small one on

Oak, and the one that shared space with a bookstore—and I liked his philosophy, which was clear, though rather spiritless and rhetorical. I suppose I was fond of him on his own account, though I can't say that for certain. He was an intelligent, kindhearted, genuine man, and not a bore, but I remember that when he confided to me his most treasured secrets and spoke of our relation to each other as friendship, it disturbed me, and I was conscious of an awkwardness. In his affection for me there was something inappropriate, tiresome, and I should have greatly preferred commonplace friendly relations.

The fact is that I was extremely attracted to his wife, Catherine Zeta-Jones. I was not in love with her, but I was attracted by her face, her eyes, her voice, her walk. I missed her when I did not see her for a long time, and my imagination pictured no one at that time so eagerly as that young, beautiful, elegant woman. I had no definite designs in regard to her, and did not dream of anything of the sort, yet for some reason, whenever we were left alone, I remembered that her husband looked upon me as his friend, and I felt awkward. When she came to talk to me about Arabica beans or told me something interesting, I listened with pleasure, and yet at the same time for some reason the reflection that she loved her husband, that he was my friend, and that she herself looked upon me as his friend, intruded. My spirits flagged and I became listless, awkward, and dull. She noticed this change and would usually say:

"You are dull without Michael. We should go get him."

And when Michael Douglas came in, she would say:

"Well, here is your friend now. Aren't you happy?"

So passed a year and a half.

It somehow happened one July Sunday that Michael Douglas and I, having nothing better to do, drove out about twenty minutes to a bakery that was making what people insisted were the best muffins in the world. They were in fact wonderful, and we stayed and tried their other baked goods as well, and when the sun set the evening came on—the evening which I shall probably never forget in my life.

After sampling cranberry and blueberry and chocolate-spice muffins, we realized it was nearly dinnertime. We had left the car, Michael Douglas's car, at a body shop for an extremely minor repair, and so we walked a short distance to a diner to get a sandwich while we waited. A few tables away we saw someone we both knew, a man named Gary Busey. He watched us carefully. Gary Busey had worked for me at my electronics store, though I had fired him for drinking, and after that he had worked for Michael Douglas, and been fired for the same reason. Gary Busey was dissolute, in look and in character. He had been a film star, and so had belonged to the privileged class; but however carefully I scrutinized his exhausted, respectful, and always perspiring face, his red beard now turning gray, his pitifully torn jacket and his red shirt, I could not discover in him the faintest trace of anything we associate with privilege. He had bright eyes and a bright smile that made as little sense as the rest of him.

Gary Busey spoke of himself as a man of education, and used to say that he had been in graduate school but had not finished his studies there, as he was expelled for smoking; then he had sung in a band and lived for two years in a monastery, from which he was also expelled, but this time not for smoking but for his weakness. He had walked all over two states, had been effectively banished from both the movie industry and the music industry. At last, being stranded in our state, he had served as a night watchman, as a groundskeeper at a park, as a manager at a dog kennel, had married a cook who was a widow and rather a loose character, and had so hopelessly sunk into a menial position, and grown so used to filth and dirt, that he even spoke of his privileged origin with a certain skepticism, the way you'd speculate about a mythological beast.

At the time I am describing, he was hanging about without a job, calling himself an independent contractor. His wife had disappeared months before with one of her coworkers from the restaurant.

From the diner we went to the park and sat on a bench, wait-ing for the car to be ready. Gary Busey had followed us out of the diner; he stood a little way off and put his hand in front of his mouth in order to cough in it respectfully if need be. By now it was dark; there was a strong smell of evening dampness, and the moon was on the point of rising. There were only two clouds in the clear starry sky exactly over our heads: one big one and one smaller; alone in the sky they were racing after one another like mother and child.

"What a glorious day!" said Michael Douglas.

"In the extreme," Gary Busey said, and he coughed respectfully into his hand. "How was it, Michael Douglas, you thought to visit these parts?" he added in an ingratiating voice, evidently anxious to get up a conversation.

Michael Douglas made no answer. Gary Busey heaved a deep sigh and said softly, not looking at us: "I suffer solely through a cause to which I must answer only to my Lord. No doubt about it, I am a hopeless and incompetent man; but believe me, I am hungry and worse off than a dog. Forgive me, Michael Douglas."

Michael Douglas was not listening, but sat musing with his head propped on his fists. The park bordered on a river, and in the distance we could see the river as it left land behind, the water meadows on the near side of it, and the crimson glare of a campfire about which black figures were moving. And beyond the fire, farther away, there were other lights, another park much like the one in which we sat. There was singing there. On the river, and here and there on the meadows, a mist was rising. High narrow coils of mist, thick and white as milk, were trailing over the river, hiding the reflection of the stars. Every minute they changed their form, and it seemed as though some were embracing, others were bowing, others lifting up their heads as though they were praying. Probably they reminded Michael Douglas of ghosts and of the dead, for he turned to face me and asked with a mournful smile:

"Tell me, my dear fellow, why is it that when we want to tell some terrible, mysterious, and fantastic story, we draw our material not from life but from the world of ghosts and of the shadows beyond the grave?"

"We are frightened of what we don't understand."

"And do you understand life? Tell me: do you understand life better than the world beyond the grave?"

Michael Douglas was sitting quite close to me, so that I felt his breath upon my cheek. In the evening twilight his face seemed paler than ever. His eyes were sad, truthful, and a little frightened, as though he were about to tell me something horrible. He looked into my eyes and went on:

"Our life and the life beyond the grave are equally incomprehensible and horrible. If anyone is afraid of ghosts, he ought to be afraid, too, of me, and of those lights and of the sky. If you think about it, all of that is no less fantastic and beyond our grasp than apparitions from the other world. Hamlet did not kill himself because he was afraid of the visions that might haunt his dreams after death. I like that famous soliloquy of his but it never touched my soul. I will confess to you as a friend that in moments of depression I have sometimes pictured to myself the hour of my death. I've invented thousands of the gloomiest visions, and I have succeeded in working myself up to an agonizing exaltation, to a state of nightmare, and I assure you, it didn't seem to me more terrible than reality.

"What I mean is, apparitions are terrible, but life is terrible, too. I don't understand life and I am afraid of it. I don't know; perhaps I am a morbid person. It seems to a sound, healthy man that he understands everything he sees and hears, but that seeming is lost to me, and from day to day I poison myself with terror. There is a disease, the fear of open spaces, but my disease is the fear of life. When I lie on the grass and watch a little beetle which was born yesterday and understands nothing, it seems to me that its life consists of nothing but fear, and in it I see myself."

"What is it exactly you are frightened of?" I asked.

"Of everything. I am not by nature a profound thinker, and I take little interest in such questions as the life beyond the grave, the destiny of humanity, and, in fact, I am rarely carried away to the heights. What chiefly frightens me is the common routine of life from which none of us can escape. I am incapable of distinguishing what is true and what is false in my actions, and they worry me. I recognize that education and the conditions of life have imprisoned me in a narrow circle of falsity, that my whole life is nothing else than a daily effort to deceive myself and other people, and to avoid noticing it; and I am frightened at the thought that to the day of my death I shall not escape from this falsity. Today I do something and tomorrow I do not understand why I did it. I entered acting, did it for years, and one day felt it was separate from me. I began to work with coffee but feel that separating from me as well. I see that we know very little and so make mistakes every day. We are unjust, we slander one another and spoil each other's lives, we waste all our powers on trash which we do not need and which hinders us from living; and that frightens me, because I don't understand why and for whom it is necessary.

"I don't understand men, my dear fellow, and I am afraid of them. It frightens me to look at most people, and I don't know for what higher objects they are suffering and what they are living for. If life is an enjoyment, then they are unnecessary, superfluous; if the object and meaning of life is to be found in economic struggle and unending, hopeless ignorance, I can't understand for whom and what this torture is necessary. I understand no one and nothing. Kindly try to understand this specimen, for instance," said Michael Douglas, pointing to Gary Busey. "Think of him!"

Noticing that we were looking at him, Gary Busey coughed deferentially into his fist and said:

"I was always a good worker and often a good man, but the great trouble has been spirits: those I have had to drink, those I have seen floating around me. If a poor fellow like me were shown consideration and given a place, I would do right by that generosity. My word's my bond."

Gary Busey was speaking passionately, and a man walking by stopped to listen. Then his cell phone rang and he turned away to answer it. That gave Michael Douglas occasion to look at his watch.

"It's seven," said Michael Douglas. "Time to get the car and go. Yes, my dear fellow," he sighed, "if only you knew how afraid I am of my ordinary everyday thoughts, in which one would have thought there should be nothing dreadful. To prevent myself from thinking, I distract my mind with work and try to tire myself out that I may sleep sound at night. Children, a wife—all that seems ordinary with other people; but how that weighs upon me, my dear fellow!"

He rubbed his face with his hands, cleared his throat, and laughed.

"If I could only tell you how I have played the fool in my life!" he said. "They all tell me that I have a sweet wife, charming children, and that I am a good husband and father. They think I am very happy and envy me. But since it has come to that, I will tell you in secret: my happy family life is only a grievous misunderstanding, and I am afraid of it." His pale face was distorted by a wry smile. He put his arm round my waist and went on in an undertone:

"You are my true friend; I believe in you and have a deep respect for you. Heaven gave us friendship that we may open our hearts and escape from the secrets that weigh upon us. Let me take advantage of your friendly feeling for me and tell you the whole truth.

"My home life, which seems to you so enchanting, is my chief misery and my chief terror. I got married in a strange and stupid way. I must tell you that I was madly in love with Catherine before I married her, and was courting her for two years. I asked her to marry me five times, and she refused me because she did not care for me in the least. The sixth, when burning with passion I crawled on my knees before her and implored her to take a beggar and marry me, she consented. What she said to me was: 'I don't love you, but I will be true to you.' I accepted that condition with rapture. At the time I understood what that meant, but I swear to God I don't understand it now. 'I don't love you, but I will be true to you.' What does that mean? It's a fog, a darkness.

"I love her now as intensely as I did the day we were married, while she, I believe, is as indifferent as ever, and I believe she is glad when I go away from home. I don't know for certain whether she cares for me or not—I don't know, I don't know; but, as you see, we live under the same roof, call each other 'thou,' sleep together, have children, our property is in common. What does it mean, what does it mean? What is the object of it? And do you understand it at all, my dear fellow? It's cruel torture! Because I don't understand our relations, I hate, sometimes her, sometimes myself, sometimes both at once. Everything is in a tangle in my brain; I torment myself and grow stupid. And as though to spite me, she grows more beautiful every day, she is getting more wonderful. I fancy her hair is marvelous, and her smile is like no other woman's. I love her, and I know that my love is hopeless.

Hopeless love for a woman by whom one has two children! Is
that intelligible? And isn't it terrible? Isn't it more terrible than
ghosts?"

He was in the mood to have talked on a good deal longer, but
luckily the auto repairman called. Our car was ready. We walked
over there, and Gary Busey followed us, and suddenly, with an ag-
grieved look in his eyes, spoke to Michael Douglas.

"Let me come back to work for you," he said, blinking furi-
ously and tilting his head on one side. "I am dying of hunger!"

"Okay," said Michael Douglas. "Show up tomorrow. Work a
week, and we'll see."

"Certainly, sir," said Gary Busey, overjoyed. "I'll come today,
sir."

It was a five-mile drive home. Michael Douglas, glad that he
had at last opened his heart to his friend, spoke cheerfully, telling
me that if everything had been satisfactory in his home life, he
should have returned to Washington and worked for a think tank.
The country could have used him, he knew. America needed new
policies; to turn away from that was not admirable. He generalized
with pleasure and expressed regret that he would be parting from
me early next morning, as he was catering an event.

And I felt awkward and depressed, and it seemed to me that
I was deceiving the man. And at the same time it was pleasant
to me. I gazed at the immense crimson moon that was rising,
and pictured the tall, graceful, fair woman, with her pale face,

always well-dressed and fragrant with some special scent, and for some reason it pleased me to think she did not love her husband.

On reaching home, we sat down to supper. Catherine Zeta-Jones, laughing, mocked our purchases one by one, and I thought that she certainly had wonderful hair and that her smile was unlike any other woman's. I watched her, and I wanted to detect in every look and movement that she did not love her husband, and I fancied that I did see it.

Michael Douglas was soon struggling with sleep. After supper he sat with us for ten minutes and said:

"Do what you want, but I have to be up at four. I'm going to bed."

He kissed his wife tenderly, pressed my hand with warmth and gratitude, and made me promise that I would certainly come for dinner the following week. He told me it was too late for him to drive me home, but that I could sleep in the guest room if I wanted rather than taking a car.

Catherine Zeta-Jones always sat up late, and on this occasion I was glad.

"And now," I began when we were left alone, "and now you'll be kind and play me something."

I felt no desire for music, but I did not know how to begin the conversation. She sat down to the piano and played, I don't remember what. I sat down beside her and looked at her long white hands and tried to read something on her cold, indifferent face. Then she smiled at something and looked at me.

"You are dull without your friend," she said.

I laughed.

"It would be enough for friendship to be here once a month, but I turn up oftener than once a week."

Saying this, I got up and walked from one end of the room to the other. She too got up and walked away to the fireplace.

"What do you mean to say by that?" she said, raising her large, clear eyes and looking at me.

I made no answer.

"What you say is not true," she went on, after a moment's thought. "You only come here on account of Michael. Well, I am very glad. One does not often see such friendships nowadays."

Not knowing what to say, I asked: "Want to go sit in the back-yard?"

I went out upon the patio. Nervous shudders were running over my head and I felt chilly with excitement. I was convinced now that our conversation would be utterly trivial, and that there was nothing particular we should be able to say to one another, but that night what I did not dare to dream of was bound to happen— that it was bound to be that night or never.

"Nice weather," I said aloud.

"It makes absolutely no difference to me," she answered from inside the house.

I went back in. Catherine was standing, as before, near the fireplace, with her hands behind her back, looking away and thinking of something.

"Why does it make no difference to you?" I asked.

"Because I am bored. You are only bored without your friend, but I am always bored. But that probably doesn't interest you. "

I sat down to the piano and struck a few chords, waiting to hear what she would say.

"Please don't stand on ceremony," she said, looking angrily at me, and she seemed as though on the point of crying with vexation. "If you are sleepy, go to bed. Because you are Michael's friend, you are not in duty bound to be bored with his wife's company. I don't want a sacrifice. Please go."

I did not, of course, go to bed. She went out on the patio while I remained inside and spent five minutes turning over the music. Then I went out, too. We stood close together in the shadow of the curtains, and below us were the steps bathed in moonlight. The black shadows of the trees stretched across the flower beds and the yellow sand of the paths.

"I have to leave in the morning, too," I said.

"Of course, if my husband's not at home you can't stay here," she said sarcastically. "I can imagine how miserable you would be if you were actually interested in me! Wait a bit: one day I shall throw myself at you. . . . I shall see with what horror you will run away from me. That would be interesting."

Her words and her pale face were angry, but her eyes were full of tender passionate love. I already looked upon this lovely creature as my property, and then for the first time I noticed that she had dark eyebrows, exquisite eyebrows. I had never seen such eyebrows before. The thought that I might at once press her to my heart, caress her, touch her wonderful hair, seemed to me such a miracle that I laughed and shut my eyes.

"It's bedtime now. Have a peaceful night," she said.

"I don't want a peaceful night," I said, laughing, following her inside. "I shall curse this night if it is a peaceful one."

I held her hand and walked her to the stairs. I saw by her face that she understood me, and was glad that I understood her, too.

I went to my room. Near the books on the table lay Michael Douglas's hat, and that reminded me of his affection for me. I went back to the patio and walked a bit in the yard. The mist had risen here, too, and the same tall, narrow, ghostly shapes that I had seen earlier on the river were trailing round the trees and bushes and wrapping about them. What a pity I could not talk to them!

In the extraordinarily transparent air, each leaf, each drop of dew, stood out distinctly; it was all smiling at me in the stillness, half asleep. There was a mound in the garden; I went up it and sat down. I was tormented by a delicious feeling. I knew for certain that in a moment I should hold in my arms, should press to my heart, her magnificent body, should kiss her eyebrows; and I wanted to disbelieve it, to tantalize myself, and was sorry that she had cost me so little trouble and had yielded so soon.

But suddenly I heard heavy footsteps. A man of medium height appeared down the street, and I recognized him as Gary Busey. He leaned against a tree and heaved a deep sigh, then lay down. A minute later he got up and lay on the other side of the tree. The gnats and the dampness of the night prevented his sleeping.

"Oh, life!" he said. "Wretched, bitter life!"

Looking at his bent, wasted body and hearing his heavy, noisy sighs, I thought of an unhappy, bitter life of which the confession had been made to me that day, and I felt uneasy and frightened at my blissful mood. I came down the knoll and went to the house.

Life, as he thinks, is terrible, I thought, so don't stand on ceremony with it, bend it to your will, and until it crushes you, snatch all you can wring from it.

Catherine was standing on the verandah. I put my arms round her without a word and began greedily kissing her eyebrows, her temples, her neck.

In my room she told me she had loved me for a long time, more than a year. She vowed eternal love, cried and begged me to take her away with me. I repeatedly took her to the window to look at her face in the moonlight, and she seemed to me a lovely dream, and I made haste to hold her tight to convince myself of the truth of it. It was long since I had known such raptures. Yet somewhere far away at the bottom of my heart I felt an awkwardness, and I was ill at ease. In her love for me there was something incongruous and burdensome, just as in Michael Douglas's friendship. It was a great, serious passion with tears and vows, and I wanted nothing serious in it—no tears, no vows, no talk of the future. Let that moonlight night flash through our lives like a meteor.

At three o'clock she went out of my room, and, while I was standing in the doorway, looking after her, at the end of the corridor Michael Douglas suddenly made his appearance; she started and stood aside to let him pass, and her whole figure was expressive of repulsion. He gave a strange smile, coughed, and came into my room.

"I left my hat here yesterday," he said without looking at me.

He found it and, holding it in both hands, put it on his head; then he looked at my confused face, at my slippers, and said in a strange, husky voice unlike his own:

"I suppose it must be my fate that I should understand nothing. . . . If you understand anything, I congratulate you. It's all darkness before my eyes."

And he went out, clearing his throat. Afterward in the kitchen I saw him standing by the coffeemaker. His hands were trembling, he was in nervous haste and kept looking round; probably he was feeling terror. Then he went out to his car and left.

Shortly afterward I called a car for myself. The sun was already rising, and the mist of the previous day clung timidly to the bushes. On my way I saw Gary Busey walking on the side of the road. He was wobbling, either from fatigue or from drunkenness.

The terror of Michael Douglas, the thought of whom I could not get out of my head, infected me. I thought of what had happened and could make nothing of it. I looked at the rooks, and it seemed so strange and terrible that they were flying.

Why have I done this? I kept asking myself in bewilderment and despair. Why has it turned out like this and not differently? Why did she have to have feelings? Why did he have to come into the room for his hat? Does it all come down to a hat?

I have not seen Michael Douglas nor his wife since. I am told that they are still living together.

THE DEATH OF A
REDHEADED MAN

ONE FINE EVENING, CONAN O'BRIEN WAS SITTING IN THE second row at the Staples Center, watching the Lakers run away from the Sacramento Kings. He was thrilled to see the game, excited and gratified. But suddenly . . . In stories one so often meets with this "But suddenly." The authors are right: life is so full of surprises! But suddenly his face puckered up, his eyes disappeared, his breathing was arrested, he put his head down, then drew it up suddenly, and "Achoo!"

It is not reprehensible for anyone to sneeze anywhere. Petty thieves sneeze and so do captains of industry, and sometimes even television hosts. All men sneeze. Conan O'Brien wiped his face with a napkin, and like a polite man, looked round to see whether he had disturbed anyone by his sneezing. But then he was overcome with confusion. He saw that an old gentleman sitting in front of him in the first row of the stalls was carefully wiping his bald head and his neck and muttering something to himself. In the old gentleman, Conan O'Brien recognized Larry King.

I have sprayed him, thought Conan O'Brien. I am not planning to be on his show anytime soon, but still it is awkward. I must apologize.

Conan O'Brien gave a cough, bent his whole person forward, and whispered in the man's ear.

"Pardon me, Mr. King, I sprayed you accidentally. . . ."

"Never mind, never mind."

"Excuse me, I did not mean to."

"Please, sit down! Let me watch the game. I'm here with Chance and Cannon!"

Conan O'Brien was embarrassed, he smiled stupidly and fell to gazing at the court. He gazed at it but was no longer feeling bliss. He began to be troubled by uneasiness. At halftime he went up to Larry King, walked beside him, and overcoming his shyness, muttered:

"I sprayed you, Mr. King. Forgive me. You see, I didn't do it to—"

"Oh, that's enough about it. I'd forgotten it, but you keep reminding me. It's like Liz Taylor," said Larry King, moving his lower lip impatiently.

I don't know what he means, but there is something fierce in his eyes, thought Conan O'Brien. And he doesn't want to talk. I ought to explain to him that I really didn't mean anything by it, that it is how nature works. I don't want him to think I spit on him. He doesn't think so now, but he will think so later!

On getting home, Conan O'Brien told his wife about his sneezing. It struck him that she took too frivolous a view of the incident; she was a little frightened at first, but when she learned that Larry King had said that it was nothing to him, she was reassured.

"Still, you had better go and apologize," she said, "or he will think you don't know how to behave in public."

"That's just it! I did say that I was sorry, but he didn't take it right. He just said something strange about Elizabeth Taylor. There wasn't time to talk properly."

The next day Conan O'Brien went to apologize. He found out that Larry King was taping a series of brief interviews with sitcom stars. He put on a shirt and tie, drove to the studio, and waited while Larry King spoke to Kaley Cuoco, Jon Cryer, and Joel McHale. Finally, Larry King stood and walked toward the bathroom. Conan O'Brien intercepted him.

"Yesterday at the game, Mr. King," Conan O'Brien began, "I sneezed and accidentally sprayed you."

"I have nothing to say about it," Larry King said. He went to the bathroom, and when he came out, he went straight over to Julie Bowen to speak to her.

He won't talk to me, thought Conan O'Brien, turning pale. That means that he is angry. It can't be left like this. I have to explain myself to him.

When Larry King had finished his conversation with Julie Bowen and was heading out to the parking lot, Conan O'Brien intercepted him again.

"Mr. King! If I am bothering you, it is only because I feel such regret. It was not intentional. Please believe me."

Larry King made a mournful face and waved his hand.

"You're just making fun of me," he said as he closed the car door and drove away.

Making fun of him? thought Conan O'Brien. That's not true at all. He has interviewed thousands of people, but he won't stop to listen to me. If that is how it is, I am not going to apologize to that guy anymore. He can go to hell. I'll write a letter to him, but I won't make any more attempts in person.

So thought Conan O'Brien as he drove home. But he did not write a letter to Larry King; he thought and thought but could not write a sentence. He had to go next day to explain in person.

The next day, Larry King was interviewing sports figures: LeBron James, Phil Mickelson, Stephen Strasburg. When Conan O'Brien saw that he was done with Danica Patrick, he hurried toward him. "I tried to talk to you yesterday," he muttered. Larry King fixed him with an owlish stare. "But it was not to make fun of you. I was apologizing for having sprayed you when I sneezed. I did not dream of making fun of you. If I made fun of you, if people started making fun of people without any concern for the truth, then there would be no respect for persons, there would be—"

"Get out!" yelled Larry King, turning suddenly purple and shaking all over.

"What?" asked Conan O'Brien, in a whisper turning numb with horror.

"Get out!" repeated Larry King, now stamping his foot.

Something seemed to give way in Conan O'Brien's stomach. Seeing nothing and hearing nothing, he reeled to the door, went out into the street, and staggered to his car. Reaching home mechanically, without taking off his tie, he lay down on the sofa and died.

A Trilogy:
The Man in a Case,
Gooseberries,
About Love

The Man in a Case

In Northern California, almost on the border with Oregon, some men went fishing and then stayed for the night in the Moose-head Lodge. There were two of them, Jack Nicholson and Adam Sandler. Jack Nicholson had been born John Joseph, a rather formal name which never suited him, and he was called simply Jack from the time he was a boy. He came fishing every year to escape the city. Adam Sandler stayed every summer at Pelican Bay, so he was thoroughly at home in the area.

They did not sleep. Jack Nicholson, a burly old fellow, was sitting outside the door, smoking a cigarette in the moonlight. Adam Sandler was lying inside on his bed, and could not be seen in the darkness.

They were telling each other all sorts of stories. Among other things, they spoke of the fact that the elder's girlfriend, a striking woman in her thirties, had never been outside of Los Angeles, had never boarded an airplane in her life, and had spent the last ten years biking from her house to yoga and the grocery store, only occasionally getting into a car.

"That is terrible but not unheard of," said Adam Sandler. "There are people in the world who try to retreat into their shell like a hermit crab. Maybe she has her reasons. I mean, maybe she's in touch with something ancient. Maybe she's returning to the period when the ancestor of man was not yet a social animal and lived alone in his den."

"Or maybe she likes waiting for me," laughed Jack Nicholson. "You can understand that."

"Who knows?" said Adam Sandler. "We're not psychologists. But people like her are not that uncommon. That's all I'm saying. I'll give you another example. Back in my early days at *Saturday Night Live,* I worked closely with Jon Lovitz. In those days, he was nothing like he is now. He was remarkable for always wearing rain boots and a warm wadded coat, and carrying an umbrella even in the very finest weather. He also kept the sleeve for the umbrella, and he had a pocket watch that he kept in a leather bag, and when he took out his keys, they were also in a little case. His face seemed to be in a case too, because he always hid it in his turned-up collar. He wore sunglasses even on overcast days and earmuffs if it was less than fifty degrees, and when he got into a cab always told the driver to turn off the air and roll up the windows. In short, the man displayed a constant impulse to wrap himself in a covering that would isolate him and protect him from external influences. Reality irritated him, frightened him, kept him in continual agitation. Maybe to justify this agitation, he always did old-fashioned comedy. He spoke in a formal tone. He watched black-and-white movies. 'Oh, no one talks like this anymore,' he would say despairingly while watching some old film noir; and as though to prove his point he would screw up his eyes and do an impression of Trevor Howard or one of those old British types. It became central to who he was as a performer. It was like his umbrellas and his rain boots, in a way.

"Jon Lovitz also tried to hide his thoughts in a case. The only things that were clear to his mind were show schedules and newspaper articles about crime, because those kinds of things helped him stay rigid and fearful. When he read an article about an attack on East Forty-first Street, say, he became clear and definite about not walking on that street at all. Whenever anyone took a risk, it made him nervous. If there had been a boat accident and I told him I was thinking of going sailing, he would shake his head and say softly:

"'Sailing seems fun, I guess. I mean, I don't know. I hope it won't lead to anything!'

"Every sort of breach of order, deviation or departure from rule, depressed him. If one of the other cast members was late for rehearsal or if we heard about some other actor who was arrested for driving drunk or if he saw a guy two-timing his girlfriend, Jon Lovitz was much disturbed, and said he hoped that it wouldn't lead to anything. At rehearsals he simply oppressed us with how careful he was, and how sure he was that everyone else's carelessness would drive them into ruin.

"He hoped that everyone would settle down. He hoped that the network wouldn't find out about this scandal or that one; that the featured player who was gambling too much would get a talking-to, or that the one with a drug problem would be forced into rehab. And, do you know, by his sighs, his despondency, his downcast face, he crushed us all, and we gave way, started to see the problems in the same way he did, and eventually bounced those people from the show.

"Jon Lovitz had a strange way of visiting your apartment. He would come over, sit down, and remain silent, as though he were carefully inspecting something. He would sit like this in silence for an hour or two and then go away. This he called 'maintaining good relations with his colleagues'; and it was obvious that coming to see us and sitting there was tiresome to him, and that he came to see us simply because he considered it his duty. We were afraid of him. Even Lorne Michaels was afraid of him. Would you believe it? We were all brave people, all young, all successful, but this little guy, with his rain boots and his umbrella, had the whole show under his thumb for years! Show? He had our lives. Our girlfriends didn't drink too much at parties for fear he'd hear of it. Under the influence of people like Jon Lovitz we got into the way of being afraid of everything. People were afraid to speak their mind, afraid to write down their thoughts, afraid to be foolish, afraid to help others . . ."

Jack Nicholson cleared his throat, meaning to say something, but first took a drag on his cigarette, gazed at the moon, and then said, with pauses:

"Yes, people can seem brave enough when you talk to them . . . but put one of those types in their midst, and they'll show their true colors soon enough . . . that's just how it is."

"For a while, Jon Lovitz lived in the same apartment building as I did," Adam Sandler went on, "on the same floor, in fact, down the hall from me. We often saw each other, and I knew how he lived when he was at home. And at home it was the same story: pajamas, sometimes even a little cap he wore to bed, blinds on the windows, bolts on the door, every kind of restriction you can imagine. He had dietary restrictions like you wouldn't believe. It wasn't that he was vegetarian. That would have been too easy. He had lists and lists of what he could and couldn't eat. And though there was a young assistant on the show who liked him and offered to cook meals he could eat, he was worried people would think it was inappropriate, and instead he searched until he found an older

man, a Jamaican guy named Clive who had never been high. Can
you imagine? A Jamaican who had never touched a joint? You'd
go over there and Clive would be in the kitchen, wearing a bright
white apron. Jon Lovitz would always mutter the same thing: 'Such
a small island, but there are so many of them.'

"Jon Lovitz had a little bedroom like a box; his bed had curtains. When he went to bed he covered his head over; it was hot and
stuffy; there was a droning noise coming from the VCR or something and a clanking from the kitchen. He felt frightened under
there. He worried about an electrical fire, or that Clive would come
in and murder him, and he had troubled dreams all night, and in
the morning, when we went together to work, he was depressed
and tired, and it was evident that the show, with all its ego and its
competition, was something he dreaded, and that even walking to
work with me bothered a man of his solitary temperament.

" 'Everyone wants to be seen,' he used to say, as though trying
to find an explanation for his depression. 'It's sickening.'

"And then the man afraid of his VCR, this man in a case—
would you believe it?—got himself a beautiful girlfriend and
almost married her."

Jack Nicholson turned slowly.

"Yeah?" he said. "Sounds unlikely."

"That's an understatement. There was a new guy on the cast,
Chris Kattan, and he had a sister, Polly. He was a short, dark young
man with big eyes and hands. He looked vaguely like a monkey,

and whenever there were monkeys in skits, he played them. His sister was taller, well-made, with black eyebrows and red cheeks, but she was energetic in the same way as her brother, always singing and laughing. You didn't even really have to make a joke, just cock an eyebrow at her, and she'd let loose with a ringing laugh. When Chris Kattan started with us, Lorne Michaels, who ran the show, threw a party. That was the custom. We weren't sure if Polly was Chris Kattan's friend or girlfriend, and when we found out she was his sister, she laughed that loud laugh like she was getting away with something. She was a bright light that season, and there weren't too many. She would dance crazy dances, sing songs she made up on the spot. She should have been in the cast instead of her brother. She fascinated all of us, even Jon Lovitz. He sat down by her and said with a little smile:

" 'Your brother reminds me of Ernst Deutsch. You know him? He was a famous German actor who played Baron Kurtz in *The Third Man*.'

"That interested her, and she began telling him that she had never seen an old movie when they were growing up, only watched television, and that since then she had started watching everything she could. She said she loved old movies from the early seventies."

Jack Nicholson lowered his cigarette and raised his eyebrows. "Old movies from the early seventies? Are you kidding me?"

Adam Sandler held up his hand. "Wait. The rest of us watched this conversation and listened, and suddenly the same idea dawned upon us all. 'It would be a good thing to make a match of it,' Lorne Michaels's wife, Alice, said to me softly. She remarked that not only was Jon Lovitz unmarried, but that he hadn't even had a serious girlfriend since she had known him. What was his attitude to women? How had he settled this question for himself? This had not interested us in the least till then; perhaps we had not even admitted the idea that a man who went out in all weathers in rain boots and slept under curtains could be in love. 'He seems set in his ways, but she seems strong enough to handle it,' Alice went on, developing her idea. 'I believe she would marry him.' The idea took hold. All sorts of things are done through boredom."

"You're telling me," said Jack Nicholson. "And most of them come in on two legs."

"Right," said Adam Sandler. "Alice was on it, and soon the other wives and girlfriends were, too, and they grew livelier and even better-looking, as though they had suddenly found a new object in life. Alice would arrange for a movie screening or a concert, and make sure the two of them—Polly and Jon Lovitz— were sitting together. Or we would throw a party and see to it that the two of them came early to help set up, or that they stayed late. She was always beaming and energetic, and he looked like he had been extracted from his house by pincers, but the machine was set in motion. We got the feeling soon enough that our efforts might not be in vain. Polly wasn't against getting herself a boyfriend or even a husband. She lived with her brother and didn't like it much; they squabbled all the time. Here's the kind of thing that happened: Chris Kattan might be coming down the street, holding a magazine. Polly would be following him, holding what seemed to be a copy of the same magazine.

" 'Why would you say that you want to go to one museum and get me interested and then switch at the last second to another?' she'd be saying. 'I'm telling you, you're impossible.'

" 'You're the impossible one,' Chris would say, thumping his stick on the pavement. 'I asked you a hundred times where you wanted to go and you said you didn't care.'

" 'Because I thought you had made up your mind.'

" 'Manipulative!' Chris would shout, more loudly than ever.

"At home, if there was an outsider present, there was sure to be a skirmish. Such a life must have been wearisome, and of course she must have longed for a home of her own. Besides, she wasn't a kid; as it turned out, she was four years older than Chris, and once at a party she told me that she had been to six weddings of childhood friends in the previous year. Whatever the reasons, Polly began to show an unmistakable interest in Jon Lovitz.

"And Jon Lovitz? He used to visit the Kattans just like he visited the rest of us. He would arrive, sit down, and remain silent. Polly would sing one of her made-up songs, or invent some crazy dance, or go off into a peal of laughter, but he would just sit, never speaking.

"Suggestion plays a great part in love affairs. Everybody—both his colleagues and the ladies—began telling Jon Lovitz that he ought to make a play for Polly, that there was nothing left for him in life but to get married; we all shoved him gently in that direction, usually with platitudes like, 'Marriage is a serious step,' that we knew would appeal to his joyless nature. Besides, Polly was good-looking and interesting; she was closer to him in age than we had first thought; and what was more, she was the first woman who had been warm and friendly in her manner to him. His head was turned, and he decided that he really ought to try for her."

"Well, at that point you ought to have taken away his rain boots and umbrella," said Jack Nicholson. "Give the poor guy a chance, at least." He laughed and lit another cigarette.

"He was already too far gone for that," said Adam Sandler. "He put a picture of Polly up in his dressing room, kept coming to see me and talking about her and home life. He parroted the platitudes back at us. 'Marriage is a serious step,' he liked to say. He was frequently at the Kattans', but he didn't alter his manner of life in the least. Indeed, his determination to consider Polly seriously seemed to have a depressing effect on him. He grew paler and quieter, and seemed to retreat further and further into his case.

"'I like Polly Kattan,' he used to say to me, with a faint and wry smile, 'and I know that everyone ought to get married, but all this has happened so suddenly. I need to weigh the duties, the risks and responsibilities. If I do this, it has to be perfect, with no loose ends, with nothing wrong. It worries me so much that I don't sleep at night. And I must confess I am afraid: her brother and she have a strange way of thinking; they look at things strangely, you know, and she's impetuous, at least. What if we get involved and we get married and then I find myself in an unpleasant position?'

"And he did not officially ask her out; he kept putting it off, to the great vexation of Alice and all our girlfriends; he went on weighing his future duties and responsibilities, and meanwhile he went for a walk with Polly almost every day—possibly he thought that this was necessary in his position—and came to see me to talk about how it might work if he had a girlfriend or a wife. And in all probability in the end he would have gone for her, and proposed, and she would have said yes, and the earth would have welcomed yet another unnecessary, stupid marriage that exists only as a barrier against boredom, if it had not been for a huge scandal. Oh, I should mention that Chris Kattan detested Jon Lovitz from the first day they met. He could not endure him.

" 'I don't understand,' he used to say to us, shrugging his shoulders—'I don't understand how you can put up with that guy, that killjoy. How can you deal with him? He's more of a drag than a bag of sand tied behind a bicycle. I will be here for a few seasons, and then I'll be off making movies, and you can stay here with Jon Lovitz. It'll be so much fun for you.'

"Or Chris Kattan would laugh a shrill, thin laugh, and ask me, waving his hands, 'What does he sit here for? What does he want? He sits and stares.'

"He even gave Jon Lovitz a nickname, 'the Snail' We didn't talk much to him about the possibility that his sister might get involved with the Snail. Once, at a party, Alice said something about how she thought that Polly and Jon Lovitz would make a good couple. He frowned and muttered, 'It's not my business. Let her marry that if she likes. I can't be bothered with other people's affairs.'"

"Other people's affairs is all there is," Jack Nicholson said.

"You're getting ahead of me," Adam Sandler said. "Listen to what happened next. Someone drew a caricature of a tiny Jon Lovitz, bearing a shell on his back, moving slowly across a landscape that turned out, upon inspection, to be a close-up of Polly's bare belly. He was going downward from her navel, and there was a caption beneath the picture: 'The Snail Trail.'"

"I like that," Jack Nicholson said. "Classy. Though when I go down from the navel I like to go faster than a snail."

Adam Sandler ignored him and went on. "The face of the snail was a perfect likeness of Jon Lovitz's face. The artist must have worked on it for hours. Copies got put in all our mailboxes, even Jon Lovitz's. It made a very painful impression on him.

"The group went out together. It was spring, and Lorne Michaels had arranged for us to take a hike just outside of the city."

"A group hike?" Jack Nicholson said. "Count me out."

"It wasn't so bad," Adam Sandler said. "Well, not for most of us. Jon Lovitz was gloomier than a storm cloud. 'People are horrible!' he said, and his lips quivered. I felt sorry for him. We drove out to the beginning of the hiking trail, and we were piling out of the car and all of a sudden—would you believe it?—Chris Kattan drove up, dressed in tiny brown shorts and an undersized red vest and a green Tirolean hat with a yellow feather. With him was Polly, dressed the same way, though much sexier; the shirt was unbuttoned low enough to show that she wasn't wearing a bra, the shorts hardly covered anything, and she wore a long blond wig over her hair. Each of them carried a giant alphorn. 'Ready for some mountain climbing, *meine schwester*?' Chris said.

"'I love to blow the horn!' Polly said.

"We all laughed. Jon Lovitz now turned white and seemed petrified. He let the rest of the group start off on the hike, and when they were a few paces ahead of us, he came and tugged at the sleeve of my jacket.

"'What just happened? Tell me!' he asked. 'Is it proper for a young woman to dress that way, and to make those kinds of comments?'

"'Hey, look,' I said. 'We're taking a weekend hike. She can do anything she wants.'

"'But how can that be?' he cried, amazed at my calm. 'What are you saying?' He was so shocked that he was unwilling to go on, and made me drive him home.

"The next day he was continually twitching and nervously rubbing his hands, and I could tell from his face that he was unwell. And he left before rehearsal was over, for the first time in his life. In the evening, he came by my house, sat silently for a few minutes, and then announced that he was going over to the Kattans. He was wrapped warmly, even though the weather was warm. Polly was out but Chris was there.

" 'Come in,' Chris said with a frown.

"Jon Lovitz sat in silence for five minutes, and then began: 'I have come to see you to relieve my mind. I am very, very much upset. First of all, someone drew a rude caricature of me and another person, someone we both care about. I regard it as my responsibility to assure you that I have had no hand in it, not just the drawings but the implication behind it. I have done nothing that would warrant that. On the contrary, I have always behaved in every way like a gentleman.' Chris Kattan sat sulking, saying nothing. Jon Lovitz waited a little, and went on slowly in a mournful voice: 'And I have something else to say to you. I have been on the show for ten years, while you have only come recently, and I consider it my duty as an older colleague to give you a warning. What happened in today's hike was shameful.'

" 'Shameful?' said Chris Kattan.

" 'The whole show is about getting attention, and there are times that it's just not appropriate. Especially for Polly. That shirt and those shorts—it's awful.'

" 'What is it you want exactly?'

" 'All I want is to warn you. You are a young man, you have a future before you, you must be very, very careful in your behavior, and you are so careless! You come late to rehearsal. There are whispers about drinking and drugs. And now this costume stunt. I'm just happy Lorne didn't see it.'

" 'It's no business of Lorne's if I want to dress that way on a Saturday!' said Chris Kattan, and he turned crimson. 'And trust me, he doesn't care. He's not the kind of dummy who goes around meddling in people's private affairs.'

"Jon Lovitz turned pale and got up.

" 'If you speak to me in that tone I cannot continue,' he said. 'And please never speak that way about Lorne in my presence.'

" 'What did I say about Lorne?' asked Chris Kattan, looking at him wrathfully. 'Leave me alone.'

"Jon Lovitz flew into a nervous flutter, and began hurriedly putting on his coat, with an expression of horror on his face. It was the first time in his life he had been spoken to so rudely.

" 'You can say what you want,' he said, as he went out from the entry to the landing on the staircase. 'I ought only to warn you: someone might have overheard us, and so our conversation isn't misunderstood, I have to tell Lorne about it so that he does not misunderstand.'

"Chris Kattan went to where Jon Lovitz was standing, just outside his apartment, and shoved him, and Jon Lovitz rolled down a half flight of stairs, his umbrella clattering down alongside him. He landed in a heap on the next landing and his umbrella came to rest right across his face. He was unhurt but lay there a moment, contemplating what had just occurred. Just then Polly came up the stairs with a friend. When she rounded the corner of the stairs, she stopped and took in the scene. She looked at his face, his crumpled coat, and his rain boots. Not understanding what had happened and supposing that he had slipped down by accident, she could not restrain herself, and laughed loud enough to be heard up and down the staircase: 'Ha-ha-ha!'

"To Jon Lovitz this was more terrible than anything. I believe he would rather have broken his neck or both legs than have been an object of ridicule. This pealing, ringing laugh was the last straw that put an end to everything. He did not hear Polly calling after him. On reaching home, the first thing he did was to remove her portrait from the table; then he went to bed, and he never got up again.

"Three days later Clive came to me and asked if we should not send for the doctor, as there was something wrong with Jon Lovitz. I went in to see him. He lay silent behind the curtain, covered with a quilt. When I asked him a question, he said only 'Yes' or 'No.'

"A month later Jon Lovitz died. Everyone from the show went to his funeral. When he was lying in his coffin his expression was mild, agreeable, even cheerful, as though he were glad that he had at last been put into a case that he would never leave again. As though in his honor, it was dull, rainy weather on the day of his funeral, and we all wore rain boots and took our umbrellas. Polly, too, was at the funeral, and when the coffin was lowered into the grave she burst into tears."

"You always want a woman to cry over you," Jack Nicholson said. "Especially a beautiful one."

"I have to say," said Adam Sandler, "that to bury a man like Jon Lovitz is a great pleasure. As we were returning from the cemetery we wore hard faces; no one wanted to display this feeling of pleasure—a feeling like that we had experienced long, long ago as children when our parents had gone out and we ran around the house for an hour or so, enjoying complete freedom. We returned from the cemetery in a good humor. But not more than a week had passed before life went on, as gloomy, oppressive, and senseless as before. We weren't prohibited from enjoying it, but we weren't fully permitted either. It was no better. Though we had buried Jon Lovitz, how many such men in cases were left, how many more of them there will be!"

"That's just how it is," said Jack Nicholson, and lit another cigarette. "I was kind of hoping that he'd get together with her. Call me a romantic."

"How many more of them there will be!" repeated Adam Sandler.

Adam Sandler got up out of bed and went onto the porch. He was a tall man with short, cropped hair, and he was less thin than he had been in the years of the story. "What a moon!" he said, looking upward.

It was midnight. On the right could be seen the ocean, stretching for miles. All was buried in deep silent slumber; one could hardly believe that nature could be so still. When on a moonlight night you see the sea, and you can't detect its movement, a feeling of calm comes over the soul; in this peace, wrapped away from care, protected from sadness by the darkness of night, it seems as though the stars look down upon you with tenderness, and as though there were no evil on earth. On the left was forest, also stretching to the horizon in the darkness.

"Yes, that is just how it is," repeated Jack Nicholson; "and isn't our living in the city, running from project to project, worrying about billing and box office, isn't that all a sort of case for us? And our spending our whole lives among trivial men and silly women, our talking and our listening to all sorts of nonsense—isn't that a case for us, too? I think I know the problem. I have a story for you."

"No; it's time to sleep," said Adam Sandler. "Tell it tomorrow."

They went into the house and lay down on their beds. And they were both covered up and beginning to doze when they suddenly heard light footsteps—patter, patter. . . . Someone was walking not far from the lodge, walking a little and stopping, and a minute later, patter, patter again. The footsteps died away.

"I'll say one thing about people," said Jack Nicholson, turning over on the other side. "They lie to your face, and they secretly think that you're a fool for putting up with their lying. You endure insult and humiliation, and can't say anything honest or true; and all that for the sake of this film or that one, or for a wretched little mention in the papers, or a nice review. It wasn't always this way. There are times I think it's not worth going on living like this."

"Well, you are off on another tack now," said Adam Sandler. "I'm hitting the hay."

And ten minutes later Adam Sandler was asleep. But Jack Nicholson kept sighing and turning over from side to side; then he got up, went outside again, and, sitting in the doorway, lit a cigarette.

GOOSEBERRIES

The whole sky had been overcast with rain clouds from early morning; it was a still day, not hot, but heavy, as it is in gray dull weather when the clouds have been hanging over the country for a long while, when one expects rain and it does not come. Jack Nicholson and Adam Sandler had been fishing and were on their way back for lunch, a trip that seemed endless. Far ahead of them they could just see the outline of the lodge, and beyond it the bank of the river. Beyond that there were meadows, clusters of trees, homes in the woods, and if you went to the top of a hill and looked out over the countryside, you could see a train that in the distance looked like a crawling caterpillar, and in clear weather even the next town. Now, in still weather, when all nature seemed mild and dreamy, Jack Nicholson and Adam Sandler were filled with love of that countryside, and both thought how great, how beautiful, a land it was.

"Last night," said Adam Sandler, "you were about to tell me a story."

"Yes; I meant to tell you about my friend Jim."

Jack Nicholson heaved a deep sigh and lit a cigarette to begin to tell his story, but just at that moment the rain began. And five minutes later heavy rain came down, covering the sky, and it was hard to tell when it would be over. Jack Nicholson and Adam Sandler pulled their jackets over their heads.

"Let's get inside somewhere," said Adam Sandler. "Let us go to the Foxx Inn; it's close by."

"Okay."

They turned aside and walked through mown fields, sometimes going straight forward, sometimes turning to the right, till they came out on the road. Soon they saw the red roofs of barns; there was a gleam of pond, and the view opened onto a large white building with a miniature golf course in front and a giant oval-shaped pool behind. This was the Foxx Inn.

The miniature golf course had a windmill on the final hole, and it was spinning in the rain. The inn was under construction, and mostly empty, though now and then a man or woman would dart across the lawn or run from the miniature golf clubhouse. It was damp, muddy, and desolate; the water looked cold and malignant. Jack Nicholson and Adam Sandler were already conscious of a feeling of wetness, messiness, and discomfort all over; their feet were heavy with mud, and when crossing the street to get to the Foxx Inn, they were silent, as though they were angry with one another.

In the main building there was a radio playing soul music. The door was open and in the doorway was standing Jamie Foxx himself, a man of forty, tall and handsome, with short hair. He had on a white shirt that badly needed washing, a weathered leather belt, and jeans and boots caked with mud. He recognized Jack Nicholson and Adam Sandler, and was delighted to see them.

"Go into the restaurant, gentlemen," he said, smiling. "I'll be there in a minute."

It was a big two-story structure. Jamie Foxx lived in a corner room, with arched ceilings and little windows. It was beautiful but plain, and there was in the whole place the smell of warm bread and cold beer. Jack Nicholson and Adam Sandler were met just outside the restaurant by a young woman so beautiful that they both stood still and looked at one another.

"You can't imagine how delighted I am to see you, my friends," said Jamie Foxx, going into the hall with them. "It is a surprise! This is Zoe Saldana," he said, indicating the woman. "Will you give our visitors something to change into? I will change too. Only I must first go and wash, for I feel like I've been filthy for months. Or else we could just go in the pool."

"Isn't it cold?"

"It's heated! You'll love it. Or else there's a row of outside showers. Whatever you want. We have almost no guests, so you'll have your privacy."

Beautiful Zoe Saldana, looking so refined and soft, brought them towels and soap, and Jamie Foxx went to out to the showers and the pool with his guests.

"It's a long time since I had a wash," he said, undressing. "I love the row of showers and the pool, but somehow I'm always working and never have time to use it."

He turned on one of the showers and stepped under the water. He soaped his hair and his neck; the water that collected at his feet was brown.

"I'm going to swim," said Jack Nicholson meaningfully. He undressed as well.

"It's a long time since I washed," said Jamie Foxx with embarrassment, giving himself a second soaping, and the water at his feet turned dark blue, like ink.

Jack Nicholson turned and jumped into the water with a loud splash, and swam in the rain, flinging his arms out wide. He stirred the water into waves; he swam to the very middle of the pool and dove to the bottom, surfacing in another place; he went from end to end without coming up for air.

"Oh, my goodness!" he said. He was enjoying himself thoroughly. "Oh, my goodness!" He swam ten lengths and then lay on his back in the middle of the pool, turning his face to the rain. Adam Sandler and Jamie Foxx were ready to go back inside— Adam Sandler had just toweled off, and Jamie Foxx was done with his shower—but still Jack Nicholson went on swimming and diving. "Oh, my goodness!" he said. "Oh, Lord, have mercy on me!"

"That's enough!" Adam Sandler shouted to him.

They went back to the inn. And only when Adam Sandler and Jack Nicholson, wearing cotton robes and slippers they borrowed from Jamie Foxx, were sitting in armchairs; and Jamie Foxx, washed and combed, in a silk shirt, a leather coat, and new black sneakers, was walking about the lobby, evidently enjoying the feeling of warmth, cleanliness, dry clothes, and light shoes; and when Zoe Saldana, stepping noiselessly and smiling softly, handed out drinks and mussels—only then did Jack Nicholson begin his story, and it seemed as though not only Adam Sandler and Jamie Foxx were listening, but also the men and women in the paintings hanging on every wall.

"I have a story about my friend Dick," he began. "He was like a brother to me. His name was Dick Miller and I saw him during the summers when my family vacationed in the country. From eight to twelve we were as close as two boys could be. Later, I got him a job in a movie called *The Terror,* and he did character work in Westerns, blaxploitation, you name it. But I'm getting ahead of myself. Let's go back to childhood.

"We ran wild in the country. We were like little wolves in the fields and the woods. We scared horses. We stripped the bark off trees. If you've ever caught a fish off a dock using bread as bait or looked overhead as birds float by in flocks, you'll never feel entirely whole in the city again. He went back to New York and I went back to New Jersey, but we both had thoughts of freedom. I liked the city fine, I have to say, but Dick was miserable. As he got older, as he worked as an actor, as he earned a reputation, he went on thinking of one thing and one thing only—how to get back to the country. This yearning by degrees passed into a definite desire, into a dream of buying himself a little farm somewhere on the banks of a river or a lake. He was a gentle, good-natured fellow, and I was fond of him, but I never sympathized with this desire to shut himself up for the rest of his life in a little farm.

"It's the correct thing to say that a man needs no more than six feet of earth. But six feet is what a corpse needs, not a man. And they say, too, now, that a man of some achievement goes back to the land, that's a good thing. But even that, it's just the same as death in life. To retreat from town, from the struggle, from the bustle of life, to retreat and bury oneself in one's farm—it's not life, it's egoism, laziness, it's monasticism of a sort, but monasticism without good works. A man does not need six feet of earth or a farm, but the whole globe, all nature, where he can have room to display the fullness of his free spirit.

"Anyway, Dick kept dreaming of how he would eat his own vegetables, which would fill the whole yard, take his meals on the green grass, sleep in the sun, sit for whole hours on the seat by the gate gazing at the fields and the forest. Gardening books and agricultural magazines were his favorite. They were like Bibles to him. When he read the newspaper, he only looked at the advertisements that had farmland for sale. And his imagination pictured the garden paths, the flowers and fruits, the trees. That sort of thing, you know. These imaginary pictures changed depending on the ad, but in every one of them he always had to have gooseberries. He was obsessed with them. There was a little patch where we vacationed as kids, and for some reason he fixed on that detail. It was the heart of everything he dreamed of, the core of what he felt.

" 'Imagine living in the country,' he would sometimes say. 'You sit on the porch and you drink tea, while your ducks swim on the pond, there is a delicious smell everywhere, and . . . and the gooseberries are growing.'

"He used to draw a map of his property, and in every map there were the same things: (a) a house for the family, (b) an area for the animals, (c) a garden for vegetables, (d) gooseberry bushes. Whatever money he got, he shut it tight in his fist. His clothes were beyond description; he looked like a beggar, but kept on saving and putting money in the bank. When he got bonuses or Christmas presents, they went into the farm account too. Once a man is absorbed by an idea, there is no doing anything with him.

"Years passed. I kept acting. He slowed down, though he didn't stop entirely. He invested a bit in a firm that sold restaurant equipment. He was over fifty, and he was still reading the advertisements in the papers and saving up for his farm. Then I heard he was married. Still with the same object of buying a farm and having gooseberries, he married an older widow without a trace of feeling for her, simply because she had money.

"He went on living frugally after marrying this widow. Her first husband had been a wealthy doctor, and with him she was accustomed to wine and vacations and little tokens of his affection; with Dick she got nearly nothing. She began to pine away in her life, took ill, and died. I don't think that Dick thought for one second that he was responsible for her death. Money, like drink, separates a man from reality. When I was growing up, there was a rich man in town who, before he died, bought honey, spread it over some cash, and ate it, so that no one else could have it. And once when I was on a movie set a stuntman fell under a train car and had his leg cut off. We rushed him to the hospital, the blood was flowing, and he kept asking them to look for his leg. It turned out there was five hundred dollars in the boot, and he was afraid it would be lost."

"That sounds like a whole separate story," said Adam Sandler.

Jack Nicholson stared into middle distance for a minute. "You shouldn't interrupt," he said. Then he went on. "Anyway, after his wife died, Dick started looking for a property for himself. With the amount of money he had accumulated—his, his wife's, the doctor's—Dick bought a property of two hundred acres in Ohio, with a main house, an area for animals, a park that could be converted to a garden, but with no orchard, no gooseberry bushes, and no duck pond; there was a river, but the water in it was the color of coffee, because it was downstream from a rubber plant. But Dick didn't worry; he ordered twenty gooseberry bushes, planted them, and began living as in the country.

"Last summer I went to pay him a visit. I thought I would go and see what it was like. In his letters to me Dick called his estate 'Miller Farms' or, in a nod to the Westerns, 'the Circle M Ranch.' I got to the place in the afternoon. It was hot. Everywhere there were ditches, fences, hedges, trees planted in rows, and there was no knowing how to get to the main yard, or where to park my car. I went up to the house, and was met by a fat red dog that looked like a pig. It wanted to bark but it was too lazy. The cook, a fat, barefooted woman, came out of the kitchen, and she, too, looked like a pig, and said that Dick was resting after dinner. I went in to see him. He was sitting up in bed with a quilt over his legs. He had grown older, fatter, wrinkled. His cheeks, his nose, and his mouth all stuck out. He looked as though he might begin grunting into the quilt at any moment.

"I shook his hand, and we laughed and cried a little at the thought that we had once been young and now were both gray-headed and near the grave. He dressed and led me out to show me the place.

" 'How are you getting along here?' I asked.

" 'Oh, all right. Great.'

"He was not a bit player any longer, but a real landowner, a gentleman farmer. He had already grown used to it and liked it. He ate a great deal, drove around in an expensive pickup truck, was suing the rubber factory, and felt important when he went into town. And he concerned himself with the salvation of his soul in a substantial, gentlemanly manner, and performed deeds of charity—not simply, but with an air of consequence. And what deeds of charity! He donated money to the local hospital, and when the local laborers did work for him, he paid them not only in money but also in whiskey—he thought that was the thing to do. Oh, that horrible whiskey! One day he might call the sheriff to roust a local man for trespassing, and the next month, if the man hauled wood for him or nailed a shingle to his bar, he'd buy him whiskey.

"Dick's life had changed for the better, and that inspired in him the most insolent self-conceit. At one time, Dick had been afraid to have any views of his own, but now could say nothing that was not gospel truth, and he made pronouncements like he was a senator. 'Education is essential, but not every man has the mind for it,' he'd say, or 'Corporal punishment is harmful as a rule, but in some cases it is necessary and there is nothing to take its place.'

" 'When a man works for me,' he would say, 'he comes away treated better than before. That is what it is to manage land.'

"All this, observe, was uttered with a wise, benevolent smile. He repeated twenty times over: land, land, land. Obviously, he did not remember the apartment in Chicago where he had been born and grown up. There was a small town named Miller just east of Cincinnati, and he was happy to let others believe that it was named for his family.

"But he's not really the point of this story. I am. I want to tell you about the change that took place in me during the few hours I spent at Miller Farms. In the evening, when we were drinking tea, the cook put on the table a plateful of gooseberries. They were not bought, but his own gooseberries, gathered for the first time since the bushes were planted. Dick laughed and looked for a minute in silence at the gooseberries, with tears in his eyes; he could not speak for excitement. Then he put one gooseberry in his mouth, looked at me with the triumph of a child who has at last received his favorite toy, and said:

" 'Delicious!'

"And he ate them greedily, continually repeating, 'Delicious! Taste them!'

"They were sour and unripe, but you know what they say: 'A man profits more from a lie that elevates him than a truth that may bring him down to earth.' In Dick, I saw a happy man who had fulfilled his cherished dream, who had attained his object in life, who was satisfied with his fate and himself. There is always, for some reason, an element of sadness mingled with my thoughts of human happiness, and, on this occasion, at the sight of a happy man, I was overcome by an oppressive feeling that was close upon despair.

"It was particularly oppressive at night. A bed was made up for me in the room next to Dick's bedroom, and I could hear that he was awake, and that he kept getting up and going to the plate of gooseberries and taking one. I reflected how many satisfied, happy people there really are! What a suffocating force that is. You look at life: the insolence and idleness of the strong, the ignorance and brutishness of the weak, incredible suffering all about us, overcrowding, violence, hypocrisy, lying, disconnection, unfelt debauchery. Yet drive through any town and look in the windows. They are calm and still. People go to the supermarket smiling, for the most part. They leave their children at school or attend our movies content to be bothered only by the trivial problems in their day, and never by the larger problems that encircle that and every other day. We get married, we grow old, we escort the dead to the cemetery; but we do not see and hear this suffering. What is terrible in life, which is as central to it as anything else, goes on somewhere behind the scenes, or in statistics: war dead, children in poverty. This order of things is evidently necessary; evidently the happy man only feels at ease because the unhappy bear their burdens in silence, and without that silence happiness would be impossible. It's a case of general hypnotism. There ought to be behind the door of every happy, contented man someone standing with a hammer, continually reminding him with a tap that there are unhappy people; that however happy he may be, life will show him the shadow of that happiness sooner or later. When trouble comes for him in the form of disease, debt, or madness, no one will see or hear, just as now he neither sees nor hears others. But there is no man with a hammer; the happy man lives at his ease, and trivial daily cares faintly agitate him like the wind in the aspen tree—and all goes well.

"That night I realized that I, too, was happy," Jack Nicholson went on, getting up. "Just like Dick, I liked to hold forth on life and art and religion. I, like Dick, used to read articles on science and play jazz records. Freedom is a blessing, I used to say; we can no more do without it than without air, but there is work to be done, and there will be time later for freedom. I used to talk like that, and now I ask, 'Why should we wait until later?' "

Jack Nicholson looked angrily at Jamie Foxx and Adam Sandler. "I know what you'll say, that work precedes freedom, that man must earn, that a productive life is important. But who is it says that? Where is the proof that it's right? You say that's how things are, but is that really the case, that I need to stand at the edge of a chasm and wait helplessly for it to widen before I ever have the chance to build a bridge across it? And again, wait for the sake of what? Wait till there's no strength to live?

"I went away from my friend's house early in the morning, and ever since then it has been unbearable for me to be at home in the city, or even to drive through a small town. I am oppressed by that peace and quiet; I am afraid to look at the windows, for there is no spectacle more painful to me now than the sight of a happy family sitting round the table. I am old and am not fit for the struggle; I am not even capable of hatred; I can only grieve inwardly, feel irritated and vexed; but at night my head is hot from the rush of ideas, and I cannot sleep. I wish I was young!"

Jack Nicholson walked backward and forward in excitement, and repeated: "I wish I was young! I wish I was young!"

He suddenly went up to Jamie Foxx and began pressing first one of his hands and then the other.

"Man," he said in an imploring voice, "don't be calm and contented, don't let yourself be put to sleep! While you are young, strong, confident, don't let yourself forget to do good, and to think about doing good, and to think about how much of life does us no good. There is no happiness, and there ought not to be; but if there is a meaning and an object in life, that meaning and object is not our happiness, but something greater and more rational. Do good!"

All the while Jack Nicholson wore a pitiful, imploring smile, as though he were asking Jamie Foxx for a personal favor.

Then all three sat in armchairs and were silent. Jack Nicholson's story had not satisfied either Adam Sandler or Jamie Foxx. It had been dreary to listen to the story of a poor old man who ate gooseberries. They wanted to talk about elegant people, about beautiful women. They counted on Jack Nicholson for that. The people in the paintings that hung on the wall were beautiful, and they had once loved and laughed, maybe even in this inn, and this seemed better than the story, as did the fact that lovely Zoe Saldana was still moving noiselessly about.

Jamie Foxx was fearfully sleepy; he had been up since four in the morning looking after the inn, and now his eyes were closing; but he was afraid his visitors might tell some interesting story after he had gone, and he lingered on. He did not go into the question whether what Jack Nicholson had just said was right and true. His visitors did not talk of miniature golf courses, nor of pools, but of something that had no direct bearing on his life, and he was glad and wanted them to go on.

"It's bedtime, though," said Adam Sandler, getting up. "We have to try to get back to the Moosehead Lodge."

"No, please," Jamie Foxx said. "Stay here tonight. Have lunch with me tomorrow. I have a few other friends coming over."

Jamie Foxx said good-night and went downstairs to his own room, while the visitors remained upstairs. They were taken to a big room with two old wooden beds decorated with carvings. The big cool beds, which had been made by the lovely Zoe Saldana, smelt agreeably of clean linen.

Jack Nicholson undressed in silence and got into bed.

"Can man ever be forgiven?" he said, and put his head under the quilt.

His cigarettes were on the table, and they had been soaked in the rain and smelled strongly of stale tobacco. Adam Sandler could not sleep for a long while on account of the oppressive smell.

The rain beat at the windowpane all night.

About Love

At lunch next day there were very nice pies, lobster, and steaks; and while the men were eating, the cook at the hotel came up to ask what the visitors would like for dinner. He was a man of medium height, with a puffy face and little eyes; he was close-shaven, and it looked as though his moustaches had not been shaved, but pulled out by the roots. Jamie Foxx explained that Zoe Saldana was in love with this cook. As he drank and was of a violent character, she did not want to marry him, but was willing to live with him without. The cook was very devout, and his religious convictions would not allow him to do this; he insisted on her marrying him and would consent to nothing else, and when he was drunk he used to abuse her and even beat her. Whenever he got drunk she used to hide upstairs and sob, and on such occasions Jamie Foxx hung around the hotel to be ready to defend her.

The men began talking about love, and not just Jamie Foxx, Adam Sandler, and Jack Nicholson, but a few friends of Jamie Foxx who had dropped by for lunch: Eddie Griffin and Katt Williams.

"How love is born," said Jamie Foxx, "why that manager does not love somebody more like herself in her spiritual and external qualities, and why she fell in love with the cook—how far questions of personal happiness are of consequence in love—all that is known; one can take what view one likes of it. So far only one incontestable truth has been uttered about love: 'This is a great mystery.' Everything else that has been written or said about love is not a conclusion, but only a statement of questions that have remained unanswered. The explanation that would seem to fit one case does not apply in a dozen others, and the very best thing, to my mind, would be to explain every case individually without attempting to generalize. We ought, as the doctors say, to individualize each case."

"Perfectly true," said Adam Sandler.

"Individualize, of course," said Eddie Griffin.

"We artistic types have a partiality for these questions that remain unanswered. Love is usually poeticized, decorated with roses, nightingales; we decorate our loves with these momentous questions, and pick the most uninteresting of them, too. When I was younger, just after *In Living Color*, I had a friend who shared my life, a charming lady, and every time I took her in my arms she was thinking how much her rent cost and if she could afford to fly back to Missouri to see her family. In the same way, when we are in love we are never tired of asking ourselves questions: whether it is honourable or dishonourable, sensible or stupid, what this love is leading up to, and so on. Whether it is a good thing or not I don't know, but that it is in the way, unsatisfactory, and irritating, I do know."

It looked as though he wanted to tell some story. People who lead a solitary existence always have something in their hearts that they are eager to talk about. In town, bachelors visit the restaurants and bars on purpose to talk, and sometimes tell the most interesting things to waiters and bartenders; in the country, as a rule, they unburden themselves to their guests. Now from the window we could see a gray sky, trees drenched in the rain; in such weather we could go nowhere, and there was nothing for us to do but to tell stories and to listen.

"I have lived out here for a while," Jamie Foxx began, "since just after *Booty Call,* I think. I am a kind of sedentary man by temperament. I'd rather do nothing than do something. But when I bought this place, there was a big mortgage on it, and as it was in the days before *Collateral,* not to mention *Ray,* I felt like I had to do lots of heavy lifting around here to get by. My body ached, and I slept as I walked. At first it seemed to me that I could easily reconcile this life of toil with my essential laziness. I set myself up in the biggest suite. I lived well in town and in the towns nearby. But one day I befriended a man who came to my room and drank up all my liquor at one sitting. It suddenly was clear to me that I needed to focus my attentions, and so I stopped going to fancy restaurants and ate more here. I became part of life in the hotel, and it became part of me.

"After a little while I started to make my way around town again, and to acquire a new group of friends. They knew me as the man who owned the hotel, nothing more. Of all my acquaintanceships, the most intimate and—to tell the truth—the most agreeable to me was my acquaintance with Jay-Z. He had been in hip-hop and then retired; he was a businessman at that point. We got along famously. One day when we were killing time, he said, 'Hey, come to dinner.'

"This was unexpected, as I knew very little about Jay-Z's personal life, and I had never been to his house. I went to my hotel room to change and went off to dinner. And here it was my lot to meet Beyoncé, his girlfriend. At that time she was still very young. It is all a thing of the past; and now I should find it difficult to define what there was so exceptional in her, what it was in her that attracted me so much; at the time, at dinner, it was all perfectly clear. I saw a lovely, intelligent young woman, such as I had never met before; and I felt her at once as someone close and already familiar, as though that face, those cordial eyes, I had seen somewhere in my childhood.

"At dinner I was very much excited, I was uncomfortable, and I don't know what I said, but Beyoncé kept shaking her head and saying to her husband:

"'Jay, what do you think?'

"Jay-Z is a good-natured man, one of those simple-hearted people who firmly maintain the opinion that once a man is a guest, he should remain so, eternally welcome.

"And both Jay-Z and Beyoncé tried to make me eat and drink as much as possible. From some trifling details, from the way they made the coffee together, for instance, and from the way they understood each other at half a word, I could gather that they lived in harmony and comfort, and that they were glad of a visitor. After dinner they played me some of her music; then it got dark, and I went home. That was at the beginning of spring.

"After that I spent the whole summer here without a break. The memory of Beyoncé remained in my mind all those days; I did not think of her exactly, but it was as though her light shadow was lying on my heart.

"In the autumn there was a theatrical performance for some charitable object in the town. I went into the VIP area, and there was Beyoncé; and again the same irresistible, thrilling impression of beauty and sweet, caressing eyes, and again the same feeling of nearness. We sat side by side, then went to the lobby.

" 'You've grown thinner,' she said. 'Have you been ill?'

" 'Yes, I've had rheumatism in my shoulder, and in rainy weather I can't sleep.'

" 'You look dispirited. In the spring, when you came to dinner, you were younger, more confident. You were full of eagerness, and talked a great deal; you were very interesting, and I really must confess I was a little carried away by you. For some reason you often came back to my memory during the summer, and when I was getting ready for the theatre today, I hoped I would see you.'

"And she laughed.

" 'But you look dispirited today,' she repeated. 'It makes you seem older.'

"The next day I lunched with Jay-Z and Beyoncé. After lunch they drove out to the lake, where they had a boat, and I went with them. I returned with them to the town, and at midnight drank with them in quiet domestic surroundings, while the fire glowed. And after that, every time I went to town I never failed to visit them. They grew used to me, and I grew used to them. As a rule I went in unannounced, as though I were one of the family.

" 'Who is there?' I would hear from a faraway room, in the drawling voice that seemed to me so lovely.

" 'It is Jamie Foxx,' answered the maid.

"Beyoncé would come out to me with an anxious face, and would ask every time:

" 'Why is it so long since you have been here? Has anything happened?'

"Her eyes, the way she did her hair, her voice, her step, always produced the same impression on me of something new and extraordinary in my life, and very important. We talked together for hours, were silent, thinking each our own thoughts, or she played for hours to me on the piano. If there was no one at home, I stayed and waited, talked to the maid, or lay on the sofa in the study and read; and when Beyoncé came back, I met her in the hall, took all her parcels from her, and for some reason I carried those parcels every time with as much love, with as much solemnity, as a boy.

"There is a proverb that if a poor man has no troubles he will buy a bad car. Beyoncé and Jay-Z had no troubles, so they made friends with me. If I did not come to the town, I must be ill or something must have happened to me, and both of them were extremely anxious. They were worried that I, a talented man with endless potential, should, instead of devoting myself to my work, live in the country, rush round like a squirrel in a rage. They fancied that I was unhappy, and that I only talked, laughed, and ate to conceal my sufferings, and even at cheerful moments when I felt happy I was aware of their searching eyes fixed upon me. They were particularly touching when I really was depressed, when I was being worried by some studio or had not money enough to pay off an old girlfriend. The two of them would whisper together at the window; then he would come to me and say with a grave face:

"'If you really are in need of money at the moment, my wife and I beg you not to hesitate to borrow from us.'

"And he would blush to his ears with emotion. And it would happen that, after whispering in the same way at the window, he would come up to me and say:

"'My wife and I earnestly beg you to accept this present.'

"And he would give me cuff links, a cigar case, or a hat, and I would send them old books and collectible movie posters I found.

In early days I often borrowed money, and was not very particular about it—borrowed wherever I could—but nothing in the world would have induced me to borrow from Jay-Z and Beyoncé. But why talk of it?

"I was unhappy. At home, in the restaurant, in the bar, I thought of her; I tried to understand the mystery of a beautiful young woman's marrying someone so uninteresting; to understand the mystery of this uninteresting, good man, who believed in his right to be happy; and I kept trying to understand why she had met him first and not me, and why such a terrible mistake in our lives need have happened.

"Sometimes in town when we ran into one another, I saw from her eyes that she was expecting me, and she would confess to me herself that she had had a peculiar feeling all that day and had guessed that I would come. We talked a long time, and were silent, yet we did not confess our love to each other, but timidly and jealously concealed it. We were afraid of everything that might reveal our secret to ourselves. I loved her tenderly, deeply, but I reflected and kept asking myself what our love could lead to if we had not the strength to fight against it.

"It seemed to be incredible that my gentle, sad love could all at once coarsely break up the even tenor of her life, of the household in which I was so loved and trusted. Would it be honorable? She would go away with me, but where? Where could I take her? It would have been a different matter if I had had a beautiful, inter-

esting life—if, for instance, I had been struggling for the eman-
cipation of my country, or had been a celebrated man of science,
or a painter; but as it was, it would mean taking her from one
everyday humdrum life to another as humdrum or perhaps more
so. As I say, I was a sedentary man, not at all the figure people saw
on screens in films like *Miami Vice* and *Law Abiding Citizen*. And how
long would our happiness last? What would happen to her in case
I was ill, in case I died, or if we simply grew cold to one another?

"And she apparently reasoned in the same way. She thought of
her husband, her friends, and of her father, who loved the husband
like a son. If she abandoned herself to her feelings, she would have
to lie, or else to tell the truth, and in her position either would have
been equally terrible and inconvenient. She was tormented by the
question of whether her love would bring me happiness—would
she not complicate my life, which, as it was, was hard enough and
full of all sorts of trouble? She fancied she was not industrious nor
energetic enough to begin a new life, and she often talked to her
husband of the importance of my marrying a girl of intelligence
and merit who would be a help to me.

"Meanwhile the years were passing. Beyoncé already had two
children. When I arrived at their house, the staff smiled cordially,
the children shouted that Uncle Jamie had come, and hung on my
neck; every one was overjoyed. They did not understand what was
passing in my soul, and thought that I, too, was happy. Every one
looked on me as a noble being. And grown-ups and children alike

felt that a noble being was walking about their rooms, and that gave a peculiar charm to their manner toward me, as though in my presence their life, too, was purer and more beautiful.

"Beyoncé and I used to go to the movies together, always walking there; we used to sit side by side, our arms touching. I would take the popcorn from her without a word, and feel at that minute that she was near me, that she was mine, that we could not live without each other; but by some strange misunderstanding, when we came out of the theatre we always said good-bye and parted as though we were strangers. Goodness knows what people were saying about us in town already, but there was not a word of truth in it all.

"In the latter years, Beyoncé took to going away for frequent visits to her mother or to her sister; she began to suffer from low spirits, she began to recognize that her life was spoiled and unsatisfied, and at times she did not care to see her husband nor her children.

"We were silent and still, and in the presence of outsiders she displayed a strange irritation in regard to me; whatever I talked about, she disagreed with me, and if I had an argument, she sided with my opponent. If I dropped anything, she would say coldly:

"'Nice work.'

"If I forgot to get her a soda in the movie theatre, she would say afterward:

"'I knew you'd forget.'

"Luckily or unluckily, there is nothing in our lives that does not end sooner or later. The time of parting came, as Jay-Z decided, as he had before, that he was not simply a businessman, and that he needed to return to his career as a performer. They had to sell their furniture, their cars, everything. When they left, everyone was sad, and I realized that I had to say good-bye not only to their home. It was arranged that at the end of August we should see Beyoncé off, and that a little later Jay-Z and the children would join her.

"We were a great crowd to see Beyoncé off at the station. When she had said good-bye to her husband and her children and there was only a minute left before the train was to leave, I ran into her compartment to put a basket, which she had almost forgotten, on the rack, and I had to say good-bye. When our eyes met in the compartment, our spiritual fortitude deserted us both; I took her in my arms, she pressed her face to my breast, and tears flowed from her eyes. Kissing her face, her shoulders, her hands wet with tears—oh, how unhappy we were!—I confessed my love for her, and with a burning pain in my heart I realized how unnecessary, how petty, and how deceptive all that had hindered us from loving was. I understood that when you love you must either, in your reasonings about that love, start from what is highest, from what is more important than happiness or unhappiness, sin or virtue in their accepted meaning, or you must not reason at all.

"I kissed her for the last time, pressed her hand, and left for-

ever. The train had already started. I went into the next compartment—it was empty—and until I reached the next station I sat
there crying. Then I walked home."

While Jamie Foxx was telling his story, the rain left off and
the sun came out. "Excuse me," Jamie Foxx said. "I have to go take
care of something over at the miniature golf course." The other
men went out on the balcony, from which there was a beautiful
view of the pool, which was shining now in the sunshine like a
mirror. They admired it, and at the same time they were sorry that
this man, who had told them this story with such genuine feeling,
should be rushing round and round these hotel grounds like a
squirrel instead of devoting himself to science or something else
that would have made his life more worthy; and they thought what
a sorrowful face Jamie Foxx must have had when he said good-bye
to her in the train and kissed her face and shoulders. A few of the
men had met her in the city, and Katt Williams knew her and
thought her beautiful.

ACKNOWLEDGMENTS

In this book, I have attempted to reanimate Anton Chekhov's great stories by pulling them gently and sometimes vigorously into the present, in part by substituting for his nineteenth-century Russian characters more contemporary figures. In acknowledging those who have helped me, inspired me, or sat patiently while I went on impatiently, I would like to reverse the process, and convert their modern names back to Russian. To Galina, and Danil, and Jasha, and Lavrik, and Borbala, and Leonid, and Arkady, and Iurosh, and Ludmila, and Igor, and Modliboga, and Kalisfena, and Gavril, and Pchuneia, and Nikolena, and Vyacheslav, and Lazzek. О своей любви я готов слагать легенды.

BOOKS BY BEN GREENMAN

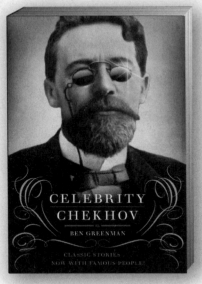

CELEBRITY CHEKHOV

978-0-06-199049-6 (paperback)

In a witty, graceful, and revelatory feat of literary reinvention, acclaimed novelist and humorist Ben Greenman takes eighteen of Chekhov's greatest stories and reimagines them as inhabited by some of the best-known entertainers of our time—everyone from Britney Spears and Tiger Woods, to Paris Hilton and David Letterman.

WHAT HE'S POISED TO DO
Stories

978-0-06-198740-3 (paperback)

A diverse and moving collection of witty, fabular, haunting stories about love, infidelity, and the vanishing art of letter writing.

"This book is like a strobe light—in short, sharp bursts, Ben Greenman renders the world we know into something startling, hypnotizing, and downright trippy."

—Daniel Handler